MORE THAN A BOSS

BOOK ONE OF THE HEARTLAND SERIES

JILL DOWNEY

More Than a Boss

The Heartland Series
Book 1

Jill Downey

DEDICATION

For Maria my dear friend
who passed shortly before I began writing this book
and
a million and one thanks to
my Mom, Sandy, Julie, and Aunt Nancy
the mid-wives of this book
whose encouragement and support became my wings

CHAPTER 1

*A*llie waited for her coffee to finish brewing as she looked dejectedly outside. *Rain, rain, and more rain.* Another dreary fall day. She sighed; any hope for a trail ride was now out of the question. As she mentally prepared her to-do list for this weekend, a flash of her sexy boss, Zane Dunn, popped into her head and she quickly squelched it. Saturdays were for leaving work behind.

Dressed comfortably in old faded jeans and a red plaid flannel shirt, she prepared to do battle with her budget before heading to the barn. Sitting at her kitchen island armed with a pencil and calculator, she punched in the figures. She always remained hopeful, but numbers never lied. She was surprised the calculator still had visible symbols on the keypad after all the abuse it took. Even when the budget looked good on paper, it never seemed to translate to real life.

Hearing the coffee maker beep, she padded over to

the pot in her fuzzy slippers and poured the black steaming liquid into an extra-large mug. She grabbed the half-and-half out of the fridge, added a substantial pour and stirred.

She plopped down on a stool and took her first sip of the morning, closed her eyes and savored the moment. The bitterness of coffee infused with cream— one of her favorite sensory indulgences.

"Well, what do you think, my friend? Aren't you glad you're in this safe warm house instead of that soggy weather?" The big white-and-calico fluffball looked at her and yawned.

Allie felt an ache as she remembered her friend Monica, who had recently lost her long battle with breast cancer. She had been a partner in crime in the rescue of Kit Kat on one of their many walks in the woods. Life just wasn't fair. Monica should be here, enjoying all the fall colors in their showy display. The fall foliage was spectacularly vibrant this year, the shimmering golds and almost-iridescent oranges of the maple trees the most flamboyant in Allie's memory. Soon the trees would be bare and there would be snow on the ground.

Shaking off her nostalgia, she reached down to scratch Kit Kat behind her ears. Her tail twitched as she stretched and responded with another yawn, then rolled onto her back, baring her round belly for a rub. Allie gently stroked her for another moment before Kit finally reached her limit and took a swipe.

Laughing Allie stuck out her tongue. "You're a brat. Don't be mean to your Mama. I'm the nice one who rescued you, remember?" Kit Kat was not only a link to her friend Monica, but she was also a much-needed companion on the many lonely nights since her divorce.

The phone rang. It was her best friend Casey. "Hello, stranger."

"Hey, what's up?" Casey said.

"Heading over to the barn this morning. I've got to clean the stalls, and I'm hoping to hop on Mel for a quick ride in the indoor arena. How about you? Anything earth-shattering happening today?"

"No, I keep telling you how boring my life is. I have to live vicariously through you and your mom."

"Sometimes boring is good." She laughed at her friend's comment, knowing Casey was the happiest that she'd ever been.

"Anything new with that demanding boss of yours?" Casey asked.

"I told you he isn't so bad. Yes, he expects a lot, but nothing more than he is willing to give. He's actually grown on me," Allie said.

"Ah, am I detecting a slight bit of protectiveness toward the boss? Maybe the sex appeal is winning out over the arrogance."

"He's not really arrogant, he's just confident and knows what he wants. That isn't arrogance."

"Well, since I've yet to meet the man, I don't have any business making assumptions. I really haven't heard you complaining about him recently, come to think about it."

"Don't read anything more into it. We just happened to find our working rhythm together, and I actually look forward to going into the office."

"Okay, I'll give him the benefit of the doubt."

"Hey, not to change the subject, but I'm planning a Thanksgiving soiree, and of course you and your family are invited." Hosting Thanksgiving this year was a big deal for Allie. This would be the first Thanksgiving in her new home. Now that she was finally settled into a home she loved and had stepped more fully into her new life, there was much to celebrate. Thanksgiving on the farm with family and friends was just what the doctor ordered. "And you know what?" Allie said. "Mom might bring a date."

"Do tell."

"I don't know all of the details, but she seems a bit smitten with this guy. His name's Pete."

"I knew it was only a matter of time. Your mom is so vibrant and beautiful, it would be a sin for her to give up on romance. Speaking of which, Charlie is still bugging me to convince you to go out with his co-worker, who, I might add, is hot. I keep telling him you're not interested, but he won't take no for an answer."

"Same answer: No thanks. I really appreciate you guys looking out for me, but right now my life is way too full and, honestly, I'm just not ready to date."

"When you're ready, you will be beating men off with sticks. You really won't need our help finding a date. Anyway, if it's meant to be, it'll happen. That's my philosophy. Who knows, it might even be the handsome boss. He's rich, sexy, smart, just perfect for you," Casey said.

"Stop it! I don't mix my professional life with my personal. I'm immune to his charms."

"Uh-huh, sure you are," Casey drawled.

"As for the fix-up, I know your husband has my best interests at heart and that means a lot to me, but the answer is still no. Now, back to more important matters. I really am freaking out a bit. I'm not that domesticated, and I need your help planning this Thanksgiving thing. I've never hosted such a big gang."

"You know I will. I love party planning. It's at the top of my list of favorite things to do."

"Good, that's settled then. Thanks. You Libras are so good at organizing. Listen, I better get off the phone. Time is slipping away, and I have a million things to do. Weekends seem to fly by, and there is never enough time to fit everything in."

"I'm in the same boat. Love you."

"Love you, too. Bye."

~

Glancing at her watch, she was shocked to see how much time had passed. If she didn't get moving, she wouldn't get anything done today. More importantly, she wouldn't get any needed horse time. She took a last swig of her coffee and rinsed out the cup. She pulled on her well-worn boots, grabbed a fleece-lined rain jacket, and headed out the door.

Allie's eyes sparkled with anticipation. Arriving at the barn, she cracked her window as she drove down the lane so she could enjoy the earthy smells of autumn and the scent of the horse farm.

Besides coffee, the smell of the horse barn was one of her favorite things in life. The tires made a crunching sound as she drove down the gravel drive. The backdrop of the beautiful fall colors, even with the gray and dreary skies, inspired her.

She parked and jumped out of her worn but dependable Subaru wagon, which had seen much better days but was bought and paid for. Not just a car, it meant much more to her than it probably should. She was quite attached to this piece of metal.

The two large barn dogs, Daniel and Jack, Lab mix rescues, ran to greet her with friendly barks as their tails wagged. Both wore expectant looks on their faces, staring at her pocket knowingly. She reached in for the dog biscuits and held out her offerings. They gobbled them up.

She laughed. "How do you do that without chewing? I swear you just swallow them whole."

They looked pleased with themselves as they turned and ran ahead, leading the way to their inner sanctum. The barn was so quiet when she entered that it almost felt like a church. She flipped on the lights and heard the gentle nickering of Mel's greeting. "Hi, big boy. I've missed you." She slid open his stall door and stepped in, latching the nylon rope across the entry behind her.

Mel rubbed his head against her shoulder as if giving her a hug; she wrapped her arms around his neck and breathed in the scent of him. That horse smell was like a perfume to Allie. She immediately relaxed. It was better than therapy, or, more precisely, it *was* therapy. The fresh pine shavings, the sweet-smelling alfalfa hay and faint aroma of liniment and manure mingled in the air to create the magic barn smell. *Literally addictive.*

"I'll be right back. I'm going to fetch your brushes. Oh, and maybe a peppermint or two for you and Jeb." She stepped out and headed to the tack room, where all the saddles, bridles, grooming supplies, just about anything horse related you could think of, were kept.

She flipped on the lights and glanced at the eraser board to see whether she had messages from either Laura or Jake, the owners of the barn. She found a big heart drawn in red marker with an arrow pointing to the small apartment-sized fridge sitting next to the board. She smiled and opened the refrigerator to spy what mystery treat was awaiting her.

Her friend Laura was notorious for her baking skills. Allie wasn't disappointed to see a huge piece of cherry pie, *her favorite*, on a paper plate wrapped in clear cellophane. Her mouth watered. Now all she needed to do was come up with dinner. She grabbed a bucket with grooming tools, a handful of horse cookies, and a couple of peppermints, and headed back to the stall.

This time she got a loud whinny from Jeb; he was fully aware that Allie was loaded down with munchies. She walked over to the beautiful paint and held out her hand with a treat. She loved the tickle of his soft lips on her palm as he searched for the peppermint. Jeb crunched happily while she returned to Mel's stall to give him a quick groom as he munched on an oat cookie.

"Did that feel good, Bubs?" She finished with the soft brush as Mel responded with another snort, followed by a soft nicker.

She *did* have time to hop on Mel for a short ride. Leading him into the indoor arena, she didn't bother with a bridle or a saddle, just jumped on bareback, using the rope on his halter and her seat to communicate. It felt great to be seated on his wide, warm back, her legs draped around him as she swayed with his movements.

Allie warmed up for several minutes, then she urged him forward. Mel transitioned beautifully from a walk into the big rocking horse gait of a canter. Softening, she synchronized her body with his, in motion together, as if they were one. They circled around several times in one direction, then switched to go the opposite way. She slowed and rode at a trot for a few minutes then at a walk for cool down.

"You are such a good boy," she said, as she leaned forward to rub his neck under his thick, black mane. She jumped down and led him back to his stall for another quick groom before turning him and Jeb out to pasture.

It was so peaceful here; she didn't miss city living one iota. Her ex was a city boy and had been insistent that they live there. She had accommodated him on that and so many other things that Allie now looked back in astonishment that she hadn't been aware of the slow erosion of her own desires.

At the time, she had thought she was happy. The luxury of being able to devote herself fulltime to her writing career had felt like a fair compromise. Now she realized that she would never live in the city again if she had a choice about it. Yet there had been happy times, which had made the end so much more painful.

Turning the two geldings out, she followed them to

the first pasture gate, opening it wide and watching as they took off at a full gallop across the field, Jeb even kicking up his back heels in sheer delight. The horses quickly settled, and soon both heads were down, grazing on some of the last of the green grass for this season.

As she finished the rest of her chores, Allie found herself slightly distracted and restless as her thoughts strayed to her boss and the defense case they were currently immersed in. It was both stimulating and slightly unnerving. They truly believed in their client's innocence, but his adversaries were very dangerous men. She wasn't sure which was more unsettling, the case itself or working so closely with her boss, Zane Dunn.

She reached up and massaged her neck and shoulders, easing some of the tension. When she was satisfied that the stalls were clean, she added more bedding, refilled the water buckets, threw a flake of hay into each stall, and emptied the wheelbarrow.

By this time, the dogs had lost interest and disappeared. She was certain she'd find them both curled up fast asleep on their beds in the tack room. She took a last mental sweep to make sure anything that should be latched or closed was, and that everything was put away. She grabbed her piece of cherry pie and, after drawing a triple heart with a big smile on the white board, turned out the lights and headed to her car.

CHAPTER 2

*A*llie had never been an early morning person, and now, coupled with the nine-to-five job, the struggle was real. She raced out the door, dribbling her to-go coffee down her black slacks as the locked door slammed shut on the strap of her satchel. She rolled her eyes as she dug for her keys to reopen the door. With the door unlocked, she considered changing, but a glance at her watch told her that was a big fat no.

As Allie arrived at work Joe, the security guard for their building, greeted her with his usual broad smile.

"How is my favorite girl today?" he asked, his dark eyes sparkling from warm brown skin.

"Pretty good, Joe. Going to your favorite diner for lunch. Do you want me to bring back a piece of apple pie?"

Joe looked pensive then responded, "Well, the thing is my wife has me on a diet, doctor's orders, but if one were to surprise me with a slice of pie it would have to remain our little secret." He winked at her with a sly grin.

She smiled and winked back. "Got it."

The elevator opened right into the huge law offices of Smith, Dunn, Rogers, and Browne. The firm occupied the entire ninth floor, with rented office space for storage of archived files on the floor below. Appearances were everything when convincing clients to entrust their lives and legal woes to a firm. The luxury implied success and inspired confidence. She always felt a slight thrill and sense of pride when she stepped into the office. The hushed ambience belied the industrious reality of this thriving law firm.

After unloading her satchel in the side drawer of her desk, she went to make sure there was a pot of coffee brewing. Someone had beat her to it, and the aroma of fresh beans filled the air.

Knocking lightly on Zane's office door, she stuck her head in to see if he was ready for a quick briefing about the forthcoming day. They met first thing every morning to go over any new cases and review pending litigations, motions, depositions, or whatever else was on the docket for the day. And there he was, all six foot of him, with his cobalt blue eyes, and designer stubble.

Ignoring the slight flutter in her stomach she said, "Are you ready for me?"

Zane gazed at her with his piercing blue eyes, crowned by dark brows and thick, almost black hair. It was a striking combination. He had already taken off his tie and the first several buttons of his white shirt were undone with the sleeves rolled up, his navy tailored suit jacket thrown casually over the back of his chair. The dark hair peeking out from the V of his shirt was sexy indeed.

A platinum-banded wristwatch contrasted with his olive skin and the dark hair on his strong forearms.

"I have to make one more phone call, then I'll be ready. Give me about fifteen minutes. Bring the Havers case file in with you. I'm a little troubled by a discovery I made over the weekend. I'd appreciate your take on it."

Allie smiled, "Don't you ever take a day off? You can't exist on work alone." He crooked his lip up slightly and began dialing the phone, effectively dismissing her.

She sat down at her desk and pulled her notes on the Havers file, glancing through them to refresh her memory. Not that her memory needed much prompting. This case was one of the most disturbing in her brief career as a paralegal.

Their client, Will Havers, had been charged as a co-conspirator in a money-laundering scheme. He was accused, along with his brother-in-law, of laundering over five million dollars for a Mexican drug cartel. Despite a vast amount of evidence that he was set up by his brother-in-law, it was determined at the preliminary hearing that the prosecution had enough evidence to proceed to trial. Their client pled not guilty and was currently out on a million dollars bail, awaiting the trial scheduled for mid-January.

Much of her present workload revolved around this case. The most difficult part for her, and she was sure for Zane as well, was that they believed in Will's innocence. She also thought the evidence clearly proved it.

Will had a beautiful wife, Camilla, and three small children under the age of five. His family meant the world to him. He had been a broken man in their initial interview. His justifiable fear of losing all that mattered had left him shattered. That Will was an innocent pawn of his brother-in-law, Christian Silva, seemed obvious. Christian, in fact, having been singled out as the mastermind of the operation, was being held without bail, awaiting trial for his part in the drug smuggling and money laundering.

Will had been subpoenaed to testify against his brother-in-law in the upcoming trial. Will's small chain of convenience stores had been a perfect cover for the laundering of Silva's drug money. Naively, Will had handed over management of three of his stores to his brother-in-law, only to be blindsided when the indictments were handed down. It had been a two-year undercover operation conducted by the FBI.

Twenty minutes later, she sipped her steaming cup of coffee and waited for her boss to look up from his computer to begin their work together. This gave her time to glance around the office, once again noticing the lack of personal mementos. No photographs, no trophies, no knickknacks. Very strange. Also, annoying, since she had a very curious nature and liked to know what made a person tick.

They made a great team. Zane usually insisted on working with her over the other office paralegal and would almost throw a tantrum if Allie wasn't available. Some of the staff were more sensitive to his moodiness, which sometimes caused hurt feelings and drama. Allie never took it personally. As she observed him, her bouncing foot was the only visible sign that she was restless.

Finally, Zane looked up. Her heart skipped a beat as he smiled, the lines fanning out around his eyes, making him seem softer and more approachable.

"Sorry, how was your weekend?" he asked.

"Pretty good, despite the rain. The best part was spending time with my horse." She reached for her reading glasses that were perched on top of her head slipping them on. "And you?" she inquired.

"Me?"

"How was your weekend?"

"Oh, work and more work."

Allie could see the fatigue in his eyes. "You look tired." She cleared her throat and said, "You were saying that you made a new discovery over the weekend?"

"Yes, not to change the subject, but do you like boating?"

"What? I suppose I do; the few times I've been out on a boat were fun. I really haven't had much opportunity. Why do you ask?"

"With the trial looming closer, I thought we could go to my lake house this weekend to immerse ourselves in the defense strategy. Maybe even get a little ahead of the case instead of chasing the damn thing. I wasn't sure if you could get away on such short notice, but it would be a paid weekend and maybe we could make some progress, for a change."

"I'll see if I can make arrangements for my horse since weekends are typically my responsibility, but I'm sure that won't be a problem." *That would be the easy part*, her senses were firing off warning signals like it was a five-alarm fire. A weekend alone with her handsome boss? Now that could be dangerous.

"We've been hitting this case hard; I think we deserve a little R and R. It is supposed to be warmer this weekend, and I'd like to get out on the lake one more time before I put my boat in storage for the winter." Zane tapped his pen against his desk, deep in thought, as if weighing and finally reaching a decision. "Let me know. I plan on getting an early start Friday morning and returning late Sunday afternoon. In the meantime, let's see what we can accomplish now." Suddenly, he was all business again.

She nodded and opened her notebook.

*A*llie's mom and Casey picked her up for lunch, and they drove to their favorite diner.

The three women huddled together in a booth at the diner, attempting to eat the absolute best French onion soup ever. It was so hot that it scalded their mouths but so tasty they couldn't wait for it to cool.

"So, Mom, have you decided to bring anyone to my Thanksgiving dinner yet?" Allie asked, curious about how Sarah would respond. At sixty-eight years young, her vivacious personality made her seem a decade younger. And after the tough transition since Dad had died, Allie was glad her mom was living again. And dating again. Even if it was through the ridiculously named "Life Ain't Over at 65" dating site.

"Well, as a matter of fact, remember the one I was telling you about, Pete? He lost his wife a few years ago to cancer and I'm the first one he's gone out with from the dating site. He's funny and sweet. On our first date we went bowling. I hadn't done that in twenty years. It was fun," she said with sparkling eyes. "If things continue on the same track, I will definitely bring him."

"Just be careful. You know I don't totally trust those dating sites. I've watched too many Dateline episodes," Allie said, only half joking.

"This site is very safe, and they vet their applicants thoroughly," Sarah said reassuringly.

"Well, I think it's fantastic and romantic," Casey said. "I hope we get to meet him soon."

Finishing their lunches, and after much discussion about who would pay the bill, Allie settled-up, remembering to take that piece of pie for Joe. She hated for the lunch to end, but she had a full day of work ahead of her, so they reluctantly parted ways after several hugs and promises to do lunch again soon.

CHAPTER 3

*A*fter lunch, there was a knock at the door announcing Will Havers' arrival. Stella opened the door without waiting, since Zane was expecting him. An extremely rattled Will and his wife Camilla entered the office. Will looked as if he'd aged twenty-five years since his arrest. His cheeks were hollowed out and there were dark circles under his frightened eyes. His normally honey-colored hair was lackluster. Camilla, a stunning woman of Mexican descent, had lost weight and appeared pale beneath her beautiful brown skin. Her speech was heavily accented, since English was her second language, so she was hesitant to share at first.

It was obvious to Allie that Camilla was heartbroken by her brother's betrayal. She begged Zane to find a way to get their lives back. "My babies," she cried. "I just want a normal life for my family. We were so happy;

everything was so perfect. *Mi hermano es despreciable*," she finished in Spanish, calling her brother despicable.

"Have you had anything unusual happen recently?" Zane asked.

"As a matter of fact, we have," Will said. "Camilla had a phone call the other day, and the person on the other end didn't say a word, just heavy breathing into the phone. It really freaked her out. Then we thought we were being followed yesterday."

Concern clouded Zane's face. "Just stay on high alert for anything unusual. I will call the police department and request that a patrol car cruise your neighborhood. Keep your doors and windows locked when you're at home and keep your phone close. If anything concerns you, call 911 immediately. Do you own a gun, Will?" Zane asked.

"Yes, I do, and believe me it is loaded and ready to fire. I have a CCW permit and no one is going to harm my family," he stated angrily.

"You and your family are my top priority, Will. We talked over the weekend about hiring a private investigator to help track down some of the players on the outside who seem to be assisting Christian. We also have a snitch on the inside who might be able to offer some help. Stay strong. Your family needs you," Zane said encouragingly.

"I know, you're right. I'll do as you suggest. Thank you, Zane, and you too, Allie," he said sincerely.

Allie was touched to be included. "You're in very good hands with Mr. Dunn. Try not to let it consume you, Will."

He fumbled in his back pocket to pull out a wallet

and flipped it open to reveal three photographs in a row. The oldest child, age four, was in the first photo, the middle picture was of their two-year-old daughter, and third was of the youngest, a baby boy, just six months old. All had their mother's beautiful dark eyes and complexion. All three were the picture of innocence. "How could you not let this consume you?" he said in anguish. "How, I ask you?"

"I don't have an answer, Will. I am so terribly sorry this is happening," Allie said.

After they left, Zane, who had heard the entire sordid story of Camilla and her brother's upbringing, shared it with Allie. "I think it's important for you to hear this. From what Will and Camilla said, Camilla and Christian Silva grew up in one of the poorest cities in Mexico. Christian, the oldest of six kids, had worshipped his mother and believed he alone shouldered the responsibility for keeping her safe from his abusive alcoholic father. As a young child, Christian had watched from the sidelines as his father brutally assaulted his mother, time and again, but had been too young and powerless to do anything about it."

"That's horrible!" Allie said.

"He swore when he got big enough, he would kill his father. By the time he was ten years old, he had become involved in petty crimes—theft, breaking and entering—stealing and pawning whatever he could find. He was determined to save his mother and family from a life of poverty. Very tragic and it gives us a little insight as to why he turned out the way that he did."

"The making of a sociopath," Allie said sadly.

"Yes. By the time he was twelve he had already

gained the attention of one of the organized crime cartels. According to Camilla, Christian was fearless, smart, and good looking. When he turned sixteen, he was officially recruited into the organization and singled out by his superiors and rose quickly up the ranks. In the early years, they tested him with small jobs, and he proved himself to be ruthless, bold, and ambitious."

"What a tragedy and waste of a life," Allie said sadly.

"You've got that right."

"I take it things only got worse?"

"Yes, especially at home. He had begun to get in between his father and his mother and had taken several severe beatings for his trouble. His hatred for his father fueled the rage in his heart and made him more determined to become rich and powerful. For the most part, his father saved his worst for Christian and his mother, but according to Camilla, the final straw was when he walked in to find his drunken father on top of her."

Allies eyes glistened with tears, "Did her father rape her?"

"He would have had Christian not shown up when he did. Instead, her brother pulled out his pistol, and held it to his father's head. He ordered him to get off her or he would kill him. Camilla was ten years old." Zane shook his head in disgust.

"Christian let him go with a warning that if he ever laid a hand on anyone in his family again, he would be a dead man. That worked for a while. Christian eventually won favor with Carlos Santiago, the leader of the crime organization, by making a competing cousin who was trying to oust him, disappear without a trace. He was destined for great things."

"Frankly, I'm not sure I want to know anymore. This is terrifying," Allie said, rubbing her hands up and down her arms, shivering.

"The story goes that the only love that Christian had left in his heart was for his mother and siblings, and Carlos Santiago. And this is where the story gets truly depraved. When he was only twenty-four years old, he came home to find his mother lying in a pool of blood, beaten almost beyond recognition. He drove her to the nearest hospital, but it was too late. She died without ever regaining consciousness. He left the hospital in his blood-soaked clothing and drove into town to a cantina to find his father and kill him. He found him all right, fucking a young prostitute in an upstairs room of the bar."

"I just can't imagine what he must have been feeling, the hopelessness and grief and rage!" Allie said.

"Christian ordered the girl to get up and leave the room. Diego begged his son for his life. Christian fired one shot into his groin and while his father screamed in agony, fired a second round between his eyes."

"Jesus Zane. How would one ever come out of those circumstances intact."

"They couldn't. Camilla was told that Christian walked out of the room and down the stairs, got into his truck and drove away. Word got back quickly to Carlos Santiago and the body was disposed of and never mentioned again. We're talking about some very bad men here. I'm glad Christian Silva is behind bars where he belongs."

CHAPTER 4

Zane really did look exhausted today. She covertly studied him as he scribbled something on a notepad.

"Zane, are you getting any rest at all?" Allie inquired.

He glanced up at her, lifting an eyebrow. "Not much. It's not unusual for me to live on adrenalin during criminal defense preparation. How about you?"

The corner of her mouth quirked up, "Not much."

"When we get to the lake, we'll try to balance out the workload with some well-earned relaxation," Zane said.

"That sounds heavenly right about now." She stretched her arms overhead and yawned. They had settled into an easy working rhythm that was pleasant and efficient. Most days lately they worked well past the normal five o'clock quitting time. Allie looked at her watch. It was currently six o'clock, which surprised her.

Noticing the time himself, Zane said, "How about

we wrap it up for the day and you let me buy you dinner?"

"I'm in." She rose from her chair and gathered up her things. "There's no way I'm cooking tonight, and the thought of another frozen pizza is less than appealing. What did you have in mind?"

"Do you like Thai food?" He pulled his gaze away from her gorgeous body, the mid-thigh length skirt showing off her long legs.

"Love it," she said.

"I know a great family-owned Thai restaurant a little off the beaten path. We'll go there," he said.

"Sounds good."

"Meet you at your desk in five," Zane said.

~

*W*alking into the Thai Bistro, they were seated at a corner table by a friendly Thai hostess. She recognized Zane, who frequented the restaurant multiple times a month. Their waitress quickly came to take their drink orders and handed them menus.

The wood flooring and subdued lighting, coupled with white tablecloths and votive candles, created an intimate atmosphere. Zane studied Allie while she looked over the menu. The pale yellow loose-weave sweater fell off her shoulders, exposing her creamy skin. The color brought out the deep brown of her eyes and complemented her platinum blond hair. A thin silver watch on her left wrist and silver bangles on her right were delicate and feminine. Her silver hoop earrings caught the light and sparkled when she moved her head.

"What do you like here?" Allie asked, not looking up from her menu.

"Everything is good. Personally, I always get pad Thai with shrimp and chicken. Their curry is great too. Right now, I'm so hungry everything sounds good. Would you like me to order for us? What if I order a couple different things and we share? That way you get to sample more than one thing," he said.

"Sure, why not live dangerously?"

The waitress returned with the wine and uncorked the bottle, pouring them each a portion in their glasses. "Delicious," Allie said. "Good choice."

"Thanks."

"Are you ready to order?" the waitress asked.

"Yes. For starters we'll have the minced chicken lettuce wraps and two crispy spring rolls, and one bowl of tom yum soup with shrimp and two spoons. For our entrees, we'll have an order of pad Thai, one order of red curry chicken, and an order of Siam beef. That should do it," he said. He smiled at the waitress, who shyly smiled back and left to place their order with the chef. They both sat back in companionable silence, sipping their wine. She glanced around the restaurant approvingly.

"How did you discover this place?" she asked.

"Stan turned me on to it," he said, referring to one of the law partners at the firm.

"He and his wife go out to eat quite a bit, don't they?" Allie asked. "We often get into discussions about food because we both love to eat." She laughed.

"Yes, he's definitely an expert on fine dining. So, Allie, tell me about your life before becoming a paralegal?"

"Well, how far back do you want me to go?" She looked down, feeling a little shy. The intensity of his gaze was unnerving.

"From the beginning," he said.

"Let's see...I spent my first eighteen years growing up on a farm. My parents were great, they let me have my own horse, Mel, who is still with me. I dated my high school sweetheart for my freshman through junior year. I was a straight-A student, a little shy, life up to that point was pretty uneventful."

"More wine?" he offered.

Nodding her head yes, she held her glass while he refilled it before topping off his own.

"And then?" He said, urging her to continue.

"Then I went off to college right out of high school and majored in English. Met my future husband the first semester. We fell in love almost immediately, engaged by the end of that year, married the following. Our parents wanted us to wait until we graduated, but nobody could tell us anything. Got pregnant immediately, lost the baby, decided that was it for me. Too devastating to think of going through that again."

"I'm sorry Allie."

"We were young and dumb. Neither of us had any experience, we were complete innocents. We both graduated and he went on to get his master's, and I initially worked part-time at the university admissions office while launching my writing career from home. After several years, I quit the university job to focus entirely on my writing."

"What did you write? Any success at it?"

"I guess. I don't know quite how to quantify my success. My first two young adult novels got published. They both had great reviews and generated some buzz. I wrote some short stories for a few magazines that were published, and I had a regular column in a local free shopper's news periodical. People sent in their questions and I gave advice with a definite humorous edge."

"You're kidding right?" Zane said.

Allie grinned. "I swear! It was quite popular."

"Go on."

"When Jeff left me, I had almost completed my third novel." She continued, "I had just turned thirty-five and thought my life was neatly packaged, bow and all. The shock and loss of him leaving devastated me."

"Was it completely unexpected?" he asked gently.

Allie glanced up at the ceiling, "That's a tough one to answer. In hindsight, there were clues. His late worknights, home less and less, no romance, which I attributed to his overworking—ha. Nevertheless, maybe I should have known, but I didn't. I trusted him with all my heart. I was completely shocked when he abruptly told me one night at dinner that he was leaving. He said he just couldn't stand one more day of living apart from the love of his life. He then dropped the bombshell that she was already pregnant, and Jeff had wanted children so badly. She was twenty-six years old and having the baby I couldn't bear to have."

"Oh, Allie." He reached across the table and took her

hand in his, the warmth of his gaze both comforting and encouraging.

"Three years ago, I would never have believed I could tell my story without breaking down, but now, I realize that our marriage was over from an emotional standpoint long before he left. We had stopped sharing our hopes and dreams. We had stopped communicating, and there was no real intimacy in the end. You know the saddest part? I don't think I would have ever left on my own. So, after clawing my way out of the abyss, I can now see how full my life is. I'm grateful for the turn it took." She smiled at Zane and asked, "What about you?" Just then, the appetizers and soup arrived.

"Saved." His strong tanned hands moved the candles and condiments around to make room for their food. "My life isn't that interesting anyway. As much as I wanted to hear about your life, I'm reluctant to share mine," he said. He smiled at the waitress as she delivered their first courses. Dipping his spring roll into a light sauce, he took a big bite and continued. "I will say that career-wise I got a very lucky break early on by defending a well-known local celebrity, and the case resulted in acquittal for my client. It was a real nail-biter, and I was completely consumed by it. It paid off in a big way by cementing my reputation as a tough litigator. Having my name and mug plastered on the front-page news everyday didn't hurt a bit." He grinned before finishing the last of his spring roll.

"And quite the handsome mug at that."

His eyes flashed then he continued, "On the personal front, I've been much less successful. I'm still a little raw and burnt from the end of my marriage. Let's save that saga for a future date. Enough for me to say mine was a very nasty and contentious divorce that left a bad taste in my mouth and disdain for the sanctity of marriage."

Allie was curious—she had heard snippets of office gossip—but his expression had become closed and she didn't want to push him to share more than he was ready to.

Zane had requested a couple of extra plates so they could sample some of every dish. The soup was just passed back and forth between them.

"Oh my gosh," she said as she polished off a lettuce wrap. This is beyond excellent. How is it that I've never heard about this place?"

"I'm glad you like it." He reached over with his cloth napkin to wipe off a smudge of hot mustard from her chin with a tenderness that caused Allie to catch her breath. His eyes were so bright and alive as if lit up from the inside. For a moment time stood still, as an awareness of one another suddenly filled the space between them.

The waitress brought their entrees, and Allie groaned at the amount of food in front of them. After sampling everything, Allie admitted that her favorite was the pad Thai, with the curry coming in a close second.

"I'm stuffed. I can't possibly eat another bite." She held her stomach.

Zane signaled the waitress and asked for a couple of to-go containers. "You take them with you, Zane, because I'm never eating again." He chuckled at her misery.

"What, no dessert?"

"I'm serious, Zane, I can't move. You're going to have to carry me to the car." The waitress brought their bill in a leather folder, and Zane slipped cash into it and offered it back.

"Do you need change?" the waitress asked.

"No, thank you. That's for you. Everything was wonderful. Our compliments to the chef and for the wonderful service," he said sincerely.

She gave a slight bow and left them alone.

It was after nine o'clock when they reached the parking garage. Zane left the car running and jumped out to open Allie's door and offer a hand. Standing close to her, he said, "Allie, I want to thank you for all your hard work on this case. You really go beyond the call of duty. I honestly don't know how I functioned before you came to work for us. You make my job so much easier. I'm more impressed with you every day. I mean that."

Allie looked down, conscious of the sudden surge of awareness between them. "Thank you."

He released her hand and turned to open her car door for her. Starting the car, she rolled her window down to say goodbye. "Thanks for the great dinner and the extra five pounds."

"Don't worry, we'll work it off tomorrow sitting in our chairs all day again. Bye, Allie." He tapped the roof of her car and got into his own vehicle. Smiling, Allie pulled out and headed for home.

Zane left the garage with a restless energy he couldn't quite define. He had enjoyed the great food, as per usual. That he found Allie captivating wasn't a complete surprise, since he'd been aware of her charm prior to their dinner out. However, he had gotten pretty good at compartmentalizing his feelings and had carefully tucked that one away. He hadn't wanted the evening to come to an end. Even after working so many hours together, he never tired of spending time with her.

This evening he found himself wanting to discover everything there was to know about her. It had been a long time since Zane had felt this way about anyone. He second-guessed himself about their upcoming weekend but felt he could keep it on a professional yet friendly basis. He also admitted that he might be fooling himself. That would be on him.

He entered his house and deactivated the alarm system. He thought he might watch a little TV before turning in, since he still felt somewhat restless.

Turning on the gas fireplace, he sank down into a comfortable recliner and clicked on the power button for the television.

He had trouble concentrating at first because his mind kept drifting back to his dinner with Allie. He had to admit that he was looking forward to their weekend together much more than he should. *Oh well, I'm not about to change it at this point.* He finally let the show draw him in and began to relax as the tension uncoiled and slipped away.

CHAPTER 5

The week had flown by. Here it was, Thursday evening already, as Allie pondered what to pack for her weekend business trip. She had to keep reminding herself that it was, in fact, a business trip and nothing more. If not, she would make herself a complete nervous wreck. Zane had advised her to pack layers so she could peel things off as the day warmed up.

She didn't really know how she felt about the upcoming weekend, beyond the odd sensation in the pit of her stomach. She felt slightly queasy, uptight. It made total sense that she would be edgy about spending time with her boss in such close proximity. It wasn't on neutral territory, like the office was. In her deepest core there was also a little anticipation and curiosity about what Zane would be like in his own element, outside of the office, after getting a taste of it at dinner the other evening.

Kit Kat decided to help pack and poked her head out from under the sweater Allie had just thrown in.

Allie chuckled. "You are the nosiest cat I have ever met, Miss Kit Kat. Don't you worry little one, I won't be gone long, and the girls will be over to shower you with love and affection." It was hard to leave her critters, but that was just the way it was. She pushed the guilt aside. Her nieces would shower Kit Kat with loads of affection. After checking the last "to do" off her list, she flossed and brushed her teeth then, wide awake from anticipation, she headed for bed.

~

*T*he next morning, after a restless night of tossing and turning, she switched off the alarm, not even bothering with the snooze button. With all the butterflies in her stomach, going back to sleep was an impossibility. She threw back the covers and rose from bed and then pulled on her robe and slippers. Rubbing her eyes, she headed downstairs to put the coffee on.

*A*n hour later she lugged her suitcase down the stairs, anxious to get going. They had agreed that Zane would pick her up at her house so she wouldn't have to worry about leaving the car unattended over the weekend.

. . .

"*A*re you trying to kill me?" Allie said. Kit Kat kept getting underfoot. "I promise it's only for two nights. Give me a break." Kit Kat ignored her and wound through Allie's legs.

Glancing in the mirror at her flushed cheeks and wide eyes she said, "Kit Kat, I look like a deer in the headlights." Kit just stared, still miffed about the suitcase.

Allie startled at the knock on the door. Zane's Mercedes SUV was so quiet she hadn't even heard him pull into her drive.

Allie opened the door and was taken aback by the raw sensuality of her boss standing on her porch in his casual attire. He wore a fitted black T-shirt and faded blue jeans. Thrown over his tee, he sported a well-worn brown leather bomber jacket. If she'd thought 'Office Zane' was sexy, 'Casual Zane' was even more so. This guy, with his bright smile, was downright dangerous. She had the sudden urge to slam the door in his face.

"Hi," she said.

"Hey." He stood on the stoop expectantly until Allie realized he was waiting for her to invite him in. She stepped back and motioned for him to enter.

Zane noted that Allie was dressed casually, in jeans and a loose, bulky sweater over a tank top. She wore her hair tied back, exposing silver hoop earrings. The usual cluster of silver bangles on one wrist and her watch on the other were her only other adornments. Her make-up was minimal; only a light pink gloss accentuated her sexy full lips. She looked fresh and young, more like she was in her twenties than her late thirties.

Stepping back, she invited him in. "Welcome to my humble abode."

He glanced around approvingly at the large living room, with its focal point an old stone fireplace. Her style was a combination of modern comfort interspersed with some unique pieces of antique furniture. The large bright sectional in front of the fireplace was inviting and just begged one to kick off shoes and snuggle around the fire. Haphazardly placed throw pillows added flare. Original artwork adorned the walls —mostly landscapes in oil, but several watercolors were interspersed as well. One area was dedicated to framed photographs of various sizes that captured, presumably, her friends, family, and pets. The room was spacious, with lots of natural light. The open floor plan allowed him to see into the dining room and kitchen as well. Her use of color was very pleasing and vibrant but at the same time gave him a feeling of sanctuary.

After his perusal he said, "Well maybe I should hire you to decorate my bachelor pad. You have a very lovely home."

Allie laughed, the ice now having been broken. "Well, true confession time, I had a lot of help. My tendency is to paint everything in neutral colors, but my friends convinced me to go a little wild." She was pleased that he approved. "Let me show you around, if you aren't in a hurry to get going."

"I would really like that," he said.

Kit Kat chose that moment to poke her head out from under an overstuffed club chair. "Who do we have here?" Zane got down on his haunches and softly called out to Kit. He reached toward her as she carefully made her way over to sniff his proffered hand. After careful inspection, she showed her approval by rubbing her whiskers against his fingers. He scratched behind her ears, which sealed the deal as far as Kit was concerned.

"Another conquest," Allie said.

"That was way too easy," Zane said.

His athletic frame rose easily from the squat, and the three of them made their way through the dining room into the kitchen, which was really the hub of the house. The previous owners had remodeled, renovated, and modernized the large kitchen space several years before deciding to sell. It retained enough of the old, but it didn't lose its farmhouse feel—aesthetically pleasing, yet highly functional.

A large island with stools around it sat in the center of the kitchen. Matching granite countertops in rich earthy tones set off by the painted white cabinets and stainless-steel appliances finished the effect. The original back door had been replaced with double French doors that led out to a deck with an arbor. Zane noticed a chimenea and covered gas grill on the deck, along with plenty of space for outdoor entertaining.

"I was lucky to get the appliances in my divorce," Allie said. "Good thing too, because I could never afford them now."

"As we discussed the other night, divorces can be brutal," he said. "I'm glad you came out okay though."

"A work in progress. Are you ready for your turn at true confessions?" she said.

A sudden cloud seemed to darken his expression. He glanced at his Rolex watch, turned abruptly away from Allie, and suggested they take off. Already striding toward the front door, he called over his shoulder, "If we don't get going, by the time we make the five-hour drive and stop for lunch, it will be late afternoon. We also need to stop by a grocery store when we get close to the lake to stock up on some food for the weekend. I apologize that I didn't have time to do that in advance."

"No problem," she called to his retreating back. Kicking herself that she had bumped into his sensitive spot, she vowed that wouldn't happen again. "I'm good to go." Bending down for one last scratch behind Kit's ears, she murmured, "Goodbye, Sweet Pea. I'll be back on Sunday." Grabbing her work bag and suitcase, she followed Zane out the door and locked it behind her.

*A*fter the initial awkwardness they settled into a comfortable silence, and Allie was content to sit back and admire the stunning landscape. Occasionally, Zane pointed out something of interest as they passed by. She liked his apparent confidence in everything he did. He maneuvered the SUV with a competency that allowed her inner backseat driver to go on autopilot. His strong hands loosely gripped the wheel, and there was a relaxed but focused air about him as he drove. *Dang, even his hands are sexy.* Tanned and large, flawlessly manicured, yet they didn't come off as fussy. They retained their masculine appearance.

For a moment, she let her mind wander into forbidden territory, wondering what it would be like to feel those same hands caressing her body. She felt a tingling between her thighs. Leaning her head back against the seat, she became aware that he had noticed her studying him. Blushing, she tried to cover up her embarrassment by commenting on the weather.

"The weather report said this weekend was going to be about as perfect as fall weather can be," she said. "I just love this time of year, don't you?"

His amused look told her that he was aware of her scrutiny but chose to go along with Allie. His eyes lingered on her lips as he responded.

"Yes, I think if all goes as planned, we'll have time to get some work done on the case and still get the boat out on the open water."

There was a sudden awareness of their proximity that wasn't present a moment ago. A feeling of intimacy like the moment at dinner the other night.

"Let's start looking for a place to pull off and have lunch. Okay with you?"

Grateful for the save, she replied overenthusiastically, "Yes, I'm starving. Are we there yet?"

Did she imagine it or did his returning smile seem like it held affection? Oh God, this was going to be a long weekend. Fortunately, several miles down the road they pulled off the four-lane and found a small mom-and-pop restaurant that appeared to cater to the locals. The place was packed. Always a good sign. After being seated, Allie excused herself to use the restroom but mostly to get a grip on her fluctuating emotions.

"Get a grip, Allie," she scolded her reflection in the mirror. Her cheeks were slightly flushed, and her eyes warm, sultry pools. *What's wrong with you? You're acting like a schoolgirl instead of a thirty-eight-year-old divorcee.*

She washed her hands, took several deep breaths, pulled back her shoulders, and returned to their booth.

"What looks good?" she asked.

"I'm thinking about a burger and fries. The waitress said that's their claim to fame."

Just then, the waitress returned, flirtatiously joking with Zane, "Well, Darlin', have you decided to take my advice?" She pulled her order pad from the back pocket of her tight jeans, pencil poised. The buxom redhead carried herself with an enviable self-assurance. Allie bit her lip on a smile. *We're all susceptible to this man's charm. Dang it.*

"Yes, I'll have the cheeseburger with lettuce, mayo, and onion. Fries on the side and a chocolate milkshake to cap it off." He smiled appealingly.

"I'll have a chef salad with lite Italian dressing on the side," Allie requested.

"You skinny ones are all alike. You've got to live a little. How about a milkshake to go along with your salad?" she joked warmly. "I'm just jealous," she said, to take any unintentional sting out of her comment.

Allie laughed and said, "Make it vanilla."

"You got it." The waitressed went to place their order with the short cook behind the high counter.

Looking into Zane's eyes, she thought she caught a brief glimmer of regret, which he quickly veiled if it was ever there at all. Spontaneously, Allie reached across the table to lightly touch his hand.

He looked down at their hands for a moment then back up at her and said, "I hope this weekend wasn't a bad idea."

Feeling slightly hurt, even though contrarily she had

been wondering the same thing, she responded, "Only if we let it be."

"I must admit that I am incredibly attracted to you, Allie. I guess I didn't realize to what extent until now, or I never would have suggested this trip. I hope you don't think less of me. I would never want to take advantage of my position of power."

Allie was touched and impressed with his confession. *Wow, an actual feminist. Who would have thought?* Of course, this just added to his appeal by about a thousand percent.

"Thank you for saying that Zane, but I'm a big girl and capable of taking care of myself and certainly responsible for my own actions and feelings."

"I know, but I am your boss. That complicates things."

"I appreciate that, and I don't want you to think that I had any ideas about this weekend. I know that your intentions for this trip had everything to do with working on this case and not about any romantic notions. Can we just acknowledge that there is a mutual attraction that we aren't going to act on and move from there?" Allie suggested.

"So, it's mutual huh?" He smiled wickedly, completely ignoring the rest of her statement.

"Be good, Zane." She smiled as the waitress arrived with their lunches, perfect timing. She hungrily dug into her salad. Having it said and out in the open was a relief.

"Could you pass me the ketchup please?" Zane said. He reached for the proffered bottle and proceeded to smother his fries under a thick, red sea of tomato sauce. "Would you like some fries?" he offered.

"Um, I would have to get a pole to fish them out. Thanks anyway." She laughed at his surprised expression.

"How is your salad?" he asked.

"Fabulous. The chicken breast is seasoned to perfection, the ham is obviously fresh baked and not just deli meat, and there are enough hardboiled eggs to feed a family of four. What's not to like? Yummy. Honestly, there are almost as many calories in my salad as are in your burger and fries, but who's counting? Not me." She grinned.

A short time later, the waitress returned with their bill and batted her eyes at Zane as she leaned over the table with cleavage in full display. Looking him straight in the eye she said, "You, sir, are a heartbreaker. Take good care of this skinny little thing and try to fatten her up a bit." Winking at Allie, she strutted away with hips swaying, to seat some new arrivals.

"Well, I guess she told me. Now I'm on a mission. Our grocery shopping just took on a whole new importance." They rose from the table and he held her coat so she could slip her arms into the sleeves. He reached into his back pocket for his wallet and pulled out a fifty to settle the bill. Allie caught herself staring at Zane's broad shoulders and gorgeous ass as he returned to their booth to leave a tip. She quickly looked away before he turned back, and as he pulled on his own jacket, they made their way to the exit. The bells on the door made a jingling sound as he opened it, and they headed for the car.

CHAPTER 6

*T*hey arrived at the lake house after buying way too much food, as far as Allie was concerned. It was enough for a whole week, but Zane assured her he would make use of anything leftover. She hadn't been sure what to expect of the accommodations, but it wasn't what she saw before her. She had thought it might be a rustic cabin or small cottage, so she was totally unprepared for the large waterfront home. It was situated on a cul-de-sac, which provided plenty of privacy. She was speechless. Now it felt more like a luxury vacation that she was getting paid to go on. *Who could have known?*

"Well then, I guess we won't have to be concerned with sleeping arrangements," Allie said.

"Oh, I wasn't worried, Allie." He raised his eyebrows suggestively with a devilish smile.

She playfully glared at him and quickly changed the

subject by grabbing a few bags and shoving them toward Zane, saying, "Lead the way, Mr. Dunn."

He just laughed out loud as he took the bags from Allie and followed her suggestion. He already seemed lighter, like all the weight he had been carrying around for weeks had suddenly been lifted.

Upon entering the main living quarters of the house, the panorama from the open kitchen, dining room, and living area was simply breathtaking. The entire wall facing the lake was windows and sliding glass doors that opened on to a massive deck. There was plenty of outdoor seating, lounges, couches, and chairs, just waiting for their colorful cushions to be thrown on. A large covered hot tub graced the corner closest to the water. It could be a home right out of *Architectural Digest.* Its location, right on a bluff, gave them an unobstructed view of the water. Zane informed her that there were stairs and a drive leading down to the private beach and the docking area where the boat was.

He made several trips in and out, unloading the car, while Allie became somewhat familiarized with the kitchen putting the groceries away. With the wine and perishables already tucked in the fridge, she began to open cabinets to stash the dry goods and spices. Zane came up behind her to help as she tried to reach a shelf a little too high for her stature. The sudden feel of his body heat against her back made her weak-kneed. When she tried to turn, she bumped up against him only to find herself facing him with about an inch between their bodies. *Oh dear.* Glancing up at his lips, she unconsciously licked her own, causing him to inhale sharply.

Placing his hands on the counter, his arms on either side, he leaned his forehead against hers and whispered, "Don't do that."

He was so close she could feel his breath. "Do what?" she whispered back.

"You know what."

With his forehead still resting against hers she found herself becoming aroused.

"I really don't."

"Licking your lips while looking at me with those liquid brown eyes," Zane said.

"Pardon me, but if I'm not mistaken, you're the one who came up behind me." She pushed softly against his muscular chest.

"Your point?"

She lifted her chin, "My point is if you can't handle the heat get out of the kitchen."

"Oh I can handle the heat, Allie; can you?"

She bit her bottom lip, "Zane…"

"Allie…"

Realizing this was a no-win conversation she said, "Well, now that the groceries are unloaded, where do I park my bags?" She scrambled to regain her composure. Anxious to put some distance between them, she retreated to the other side of the room to grab her things. "I'd like to call my mom to let her know I've made it safely and also to freshen up a bit." Secretly, she felt like she was running from a firestorm. Unfortunately, that storm resided within, so there would be no escape.

After splashing her face with some cold water and making her phone calls, she felt more like herself. Now she had a chance to study her surroundings. Much like the rest of the house, her room was pure luxury. An inviting king-sized sleigh bed with a cream-colored duvet was topped with a half-dozen pillows of assorted sizes, patterns and colors. There was a matching soft cream shag rug over cherry hardwood floors. The large window provided a view of the wooded lot adjacent to the house.

There was an *en suite* adjoining the bedroom that was practically as big as her guest bedroom at the farmhouse. The double walk-in shower had white tiles from floor to ceiling and a his-and-her white marble sink with a full mirror behind running the length of the wall. The bath had all the latest bathroom fixtures, of course. Sumptuous white towels hung from racks, with extras neatly folded on shelving. The dark navy tiled floor appeared to be heated, as she spied the wall switch to activate that feature. It wouldn't be hard to get used to this.

How in the heck did she ever think that Zane Dunn was aloof? He was all smoldering embers under that calm exterior. Out of the office environment, he was revealing a much more dynamic side that up until now she'd only caught glimpses of. He wasn't all brains, looks, and bossiness. He was displaying a carefree side. She would even go as far as to say he was fun to be with. She was still trying to wrap her mind around this information when her cellphone started chirping.

The screen said it was a private number, but she answered anyway. "Hello?"

She strained to hear the person on the other end, but she just heard heavy breathing. "Hello?" she said again.

Still no response. A chill went down her spine. She gave it one more try before hanging up. *Shake it off girl. Wrong number obviously.* Yet she still had a vague sense of uneasiness as she made her way back to Zane, remembering that Camilla had received a similar call.

"What's wrong, Allie? You look like you've seen a ghost." Concern etched his features.

"I just had a prank call. I'm sure it was just a wrong number, but the breathing rattled me a bit," she admitted.

"Did the caller say anything?"

"No, that's the thing. I answered and said hello three times, but all I could hear was heavy breathing, so I hung up. Of course, it said private caller on the ID." Frowning, she said, "Can we change the subject? I've got the jitters." Rubbing her hands up and down her arms, she tried to shake off her sense of fear.

His jaw tightened, "Just like the call Will and Camilla received. Look, Allie, I need to know if anything like this happens now or in the future. Remember—and I'm not trying to frighten you—we're working on a big case with some very bad men. As I told the Havers, I would feel a whole lot better if I knew you kept me informed about any threats, whether real or imagined." He walked over to her and gave her a brief hug and ruffled her hair, which had worked free of its elastic band a long time ago. "Promise me?" he asked softly, rubbing the pad of his thumb over her cheek.

"I promise." She looked up at him through her long, dark lashes.

He fought the urge to pull her into his arms and put his lips to her hair. His voice gruff, he said "God, Allie, the thought of anyone threatening you makes me feel a little crazy. Please be careful and stay safe."

"Zane, you're scaring me. Please it was just one phone call. I'll be careful, but can we talk about something else?"

With effort, he changed the subject and opened the fridge, grabbing one of the bottles of wine and twisting off the cap. "I don't know about you, but for me, a pre-dinner glass of wine is in order. I think we've earned it."

"Yes please."

"Let's just settle in tonight, cook together, turn in early, and start working on the case tomorrow morning." With that, he took two wine glasses from the open shelf and poured a generous amount of sauvignon blanc into each glass.

"You're the boss." She gratefully accepted the wine and moved over to the couch, sitting and curling her feet beneath her.

Zane took a seat next to her. "I'd love to hear more about you Allie... about your family, your horse, your life. What's your favorite color...your favorite movie?" he asked.

"Whoa." She laughed, and her gaze softened. "I know what you're trying to do Zane Dunn, and it's working. Thank you. I'm feeling better already. Okay, so one of my favorite movies is *A Star is Born*, the Judy Garland version. Favorite color depends on my mood. How about you?"

"Film: *The Wrestler*. Very powerful movie. Stayed with me for days. Color: blue," he said.

"Are you hungry yet?" Allie asked, suddenly starving.

"Is that all you think about, 'Skinny'?" he teased.

"Only when my stomach is growling so loud that I can't hear my own voice. What did you have in mind for dinner tonight?" she asked.

"I was thinking about making a fresh basil pesto and tossing it with the bow-tie pasta and the pine nuts we bought today. I'll fire up the grill and throw those chicken breasts on. I have a poultry dry rub I'll use. I can toss a salad as well. How does that sound to you?"

"Perfect." She tried to sound enthused, but that jittery feeling had returned. She rose from the couch and began to help, needing the distraction. "I'll start chopping the garlic."

"Just peel it, the food processor will do the rest. And Allie," she turned toward him, "It will be okay. I won't let anything happen to you."

And, just like that, her fear disappeared because she believed him.

"But first, a little atmosphere," he said. "Van Morrison or Etta James? Your call," he tossed over his shoulder as he walked toward the living room.

"I love them both," she said. "How about we start with Etta James while we are cooking, then Van Morrison later."

Bending over a shelf, he studied his extensive album collection until he found what he was looking for.

"Here it is," he smiled with satisfaction. Taking the vinyl disc out of its sleeve, he pulled up the stylus so he could place the album on the platter, then carefully placed the needle on the spinning record. Suddenly, Etta James' smooth, unmistakable voice filled the room. The sound system was obviously top of the line. She had never heard such great sound that wasn't live.

"Wow, I'm impressed. You're full of surprises. My parents were big fans of jazz and blues. I used to watch my dad whisk my mom around the kitchen floor to Nancy Wilson and Etta James tunes. It was so romantic. I always dreamed that one day I would have a love as great as theirs. You know, they never lost the romance. Even when my dad was dying, they still looked at each other like newlyweds." Her eyes moistened as a wave of nostalgia and longing for those days washed over her.

Not wanting to put a damper on the evening, she quickly followed with, "And a turntable? I mean wow, really? In a funny way you are ahead of your time." She laughed, her back still to him peeling the garlic. "Records are making a comeback in a big way. So it's old fashioned but actually cutting edge all at the same time. How hip is that?" she teased.

"I know, I'm a bit of a music geek, but I never got rid of my albums, and I never thought the music sounded as good on a CD player. It just wasn't the same." He walked back to the kitchen toward Allie.

He took the knife out of her hand and set his wine on the counter. "Come here you. We can't possibly let Etta's song play on without a dance." He looked down at her surprised expression and pulled her close into his arms, gently swaying to *"At Last."* At first Allie tensed up, but finally she gave in to the music and the moment. She could worry about the rest later. Resting her head on his broad shoulder, she released her held breath and let herself be carried away. The feel of his body pressed against the length of her own, intoxicated her with its sensuality.

He sang some of the words quietly as he expertly

guided her around the dining room floor. He crooned softly about blue skies and clover. As he picked up steam, he began to sing full-on, twirling her around, her back arched as he lowered her toward the floor. Her full breasts looked ready to burst from the confines of her clothing. She began to laugh out loud with sheer joy. Continuing, now that he knew he had a captive audience, he began to ham it up a little more, singing about smiles and casting spells as he dipped and twirled her. Finally, he claimed that she was his at last, with another playful dip. By this time, she was giggling so much that her belly hurt.

The song ended, and Allie exclaimed, "Oh, Zane, I haven't laughed that hard in I can't remember when. I love this lighter side of you. Thank you for that. You've got the moves; I'll give you that. You don't sing half bad either. Is there anything you *can't* do?"

By this time, the upbeat song *"Something's Got a Hold of Me"* was playing. Without answering, eyes twinkling with mischief, he started dancing again in an exaggerated way, still holding on to her hand while doing the twist, winding almost all the way to the ground and back up again.

"Stop. I can't take anymore. My belly hurts." She wiped the tears from her eyes as he lifted her up off the ground in a bear hug and swung her around in a circle before carefully placing her feet back on the floor.

Like a switch had been flipped, they became aware of the electricity surging between them. He raised her hand to his lips, turned her palm face up, and gently kissed the soft skin on the inside of her wrist. He worked his way to the flesh of her palm, which sent shivers up Allie's spine. He studied the hand he held, so small and delicate in contrast to his own. Raising his head, his eyes smoldered with desire. Rather than releasing her hand, he led her back to the kitchen counter, picked up the knife, wrapped her long, slender fingers around the handle, and returned to his wine.

Over dinner, they chatted about their childhoods, the pets they had growing up, their friends and family, all safe subjects that wouldn't get Allie into trouble again. They discovered that they had quite a bit in common. They both loved music and the outdoors, good films, especially the classics; they both thought they were somewhat of a throwback to a bygone era and were okay with that. They both liked to cook and enjoyed good food.

After Zane's earlier response, Allie stayed well away from his personal life. She was curious to know what his ex-wife was like, but she held her tongue. If he wanted to share that with her, he would, and it would be on his timetable and terms, not hers. She could wait for it.

After dinner, they played one game of Scrabble before bed. They had both been yawning for the last half hour and knew they had work to do the following day. Allie rinsed out their wine glasses and placed them in the drainer. Zane had loaded the dishwasher earlier and it was on the dry cycle now.

"Zane, I don't know how to thank you for such a lovely evening. It really was perfect." She smiled at him shyly.

"I'm the lucky one. I got to spend the evening with a beautiful, interesting woman, who also happens to be a fantastic dancer and the bonus is that she thinks I'm funny," he said lightly and winked. "Goodnight, Allie. Sweet dreams."

"Night, Zane."

Allie would have been lying to herself if she didn't admit to feelings of disappointment that Zane hadn't kissed her goodnight. It was slightly confusing. It seemed like a natural progression of the evening. However, she knew it was for the best. Things had moved a little too fast, and he was her boss, after all.

Now, standing in her cream silk PJs in the humongous bathroom, Allie studied her face in the mirror, looking for outer signs reflecting her inner conflict. Nope, other than the dark smudges under her eyes from fatigue, she looked basically the same as she did yesterday. Hard to believe. She felt like she had just lived about three months in one day. She washed her face, brushed and flossed her teeth, feeling more balanced than she had since yesterday. The nightly routine quieted her inner turmoil.

She jumped onto the massive bed and snuggled under the comforter. She reached over and switched off the lamp, too tired to even attempt to read. Allie was asleep before her head hit the pillow.

CHAPTER 7

*A*llie woke up to the unmistakable aroma of bacon frying. Slipping out of bed, she reached for her robe and padded down the hall to investigate. "Mmm, something smells good. I hope you are planning to share, considering that you have standing orders from our server," she said.

"I think a pound of bacon will feed the two of us, what do you think?" Zane smiled as he used a fork to turn the bacon. "Did you sleep well?"

"I don't think I even moved from the position I fell asleep in. In other words, I slept like a log. Anything I can do to help with breakfast?"

"No, I have it under control. Should be about another ten minutes and it will be chow time. How do you like your eggs?"

"Sunny-side up. Okay then, I'll go get dressed," she said.

"Don't do it on my account." He loved seeing Allie all

sleep-tousled in her oversized fluffy robe. Her disheveled hair was loose from its usual hairband. Even without any makeup, she was a knockout. His vow to keep things on a more professional level the rest of the weekend was going to prove difficult, but he felt he had to try. Seeing her like this was challenging his earlier pledge to himself in a big way. "You could wait until after breakfast. Why don't you just pull up a stool and keep me company."

"Perfect," she said. He set a plate in front of her piled high with bacon, two pieces of toast, and two eggs. "You really didn't have to take our waitress's advice literally, but I'm not complaining either." She used her toast to sop up the runny egg yolk. "Mmm, this is delicious," she took a big mouthful, giggling, she quickly wiped the egg dripping down her chin before it ended up on her chest. She leaned further over her plate, attempting to avoid making a mess. Zane handed her another napkin and sat next to her to eat his full plate of food. In no time, Allie was polishing off the last bite.

"There's more bacon," Zane tempted her.

"You're kidding, right? I am stuffed but thank you." She rose to rinse off her plate and opened the dishwasher. Seeing that Zane had already unloaded the previous day's dishes, she stuck her plate on the rack, impressed with this domestic side of him.

"Can we talk for a minute before you shower and dress?" Zane asked.

"Sure, what's up?" she asked curiously. This morning, although Zane had been pleasant and warm, he had most definitely dialed down the sexual energy of last night. She had kind of expected it and agreed that it was the wiser course for them to take. They could still be friends, but they needed to keep their work relationship at the forefront.

"Allie, about last night, I feel like I owe you an apology. I probably got carried away. It's just that I'm incredibly attracted to you, but I'll try my best to keep a lid on it. We've both been burnt in our divorces, and I'm not sure that my baggage has been entirely dealt with. You're too special to have anything but one hundred percent."

Holding up her hand, Allie said, "Zane, wait, you don't have to say more. I agree with you. That we have a strong attraction to one another is obvious, but the timing is all wrong. Let's just move forward from here as friends. It'll make working together much simpler. I don't want you to take this all on yourself. I was all-in last night every bit as much as you were." She reached for his hand and held it lightly. "Friends?" she asked softly.

"Friends, dammit," he replied gruffly.

"Alrighty then. I'll go shower, dress, then report to you." She raised her hand in a mock salute, "Ready for work, Mr. Dunn."

He smiled lopsidedly at her and shook his head. "This is going to be interesting"

Allie shrugged as she replied, "I've always been up for a good challenge." *The odds are not in our favor.*

*F*ive hours later, after bouncing around different ideas and strategies, they had made some progress and decided to call it quits for the day. Allie had pages of notes to show for their efforts. They had some differing opinions for the best plan of action but agreed that the case looked good for their client.

Zane was determined to take the boat out one last time for the season. The weather cooperated, with bright sunny skies and temperatures hovering around seventy degrees. Tomorrow, he would trailer the boat to his storage unit for safekeeping over the winter.

"Dress warmly, the air over the water will be cooler."

"Aye aye, Captain, I'll be right back." She headed to her bedroom and stripped down so that she could add a few layers of clothing. Long jeans, camisole, long-sleeve tee, jacket, and scarf. That ought to do it. She threw on her old pair of sneakers and returned to the kitchen.

Zane was ready and waiting, so they made their way down the steep stone staircase to the boat dock below. He held her hand as she awkwardly stepped up and into the swaying boat. He untied the vessel, threw in the rope, and agilely jumped aboard. Climbing into the captain's seat, he started the motor and slowly cruised out of the no-wake zone, away from shore.

After he was a safe distance out, he gunned the motor and opened the engine to full throttle. The combination of speed, wind, air, and water were exhilarating. It felt like a purification of her spirit. With eyes closed, Allie raised her face to the sun as her long hair whipped behind her. She loved the sense of power surging through her. It made her feel carefree, daring, downright adventurous. From her seat next to Zane she had a great view of him. She glanced over, once again marveling at his competency and power. He was in his element, virile, strong, and completely at ease. He was most definitely a force of nature.

They didn't bother with conversation because trying to hear over the engine would have been futile. It was enough just to share the sheer thrill of the ride. Zane began to slow the craft and came to a stop, turning off the motor. After dropping anchor, they relaxed companionably, enjoying the rocking motion and the sound of water lapping against the hull. Without the wind, they were able to remove their jackets and lean back and soak up some rays of sun. It was great to just be. After their mental exertion today, they needed a break from thinking. Time passed easily, and the day sky began to dim.

"Time to turn back," he announced. With his navigation lights on, he turned and headed back to the dock. By the time they arrived, the stars were beginning to pop out. With no light pollution, they seemed close enough to touch. He threw the rope around a deck post until he could secure it to the cleat hitch. His lithe body had no trouble jumping down onto the deck. He turned to help Allie out of the boat. Gripping her around the waist, he easily lifted her down beside him. She took a moment to gaze at the twinkling sky, marveling at how many more stars there seemed to be here without any light interference.

"You go on ahead to the house while I finish up here. Catch," he said, tossing the keys in the air. She snatched them before they dropped to the ground. "Here's a flashlight. I'll be right up."

"Are you sure I can't help?" she asked.

"Nope, I could do this in my sleep. Thanks."

Neither felt like cooking, so they agreed on cheese, hummus, sliced pepperoni, and prosciutto with crackers for dinner. They lit a small fire in the chimenea and pulled their chairs up close to the warmth. Zane put the plate of food on the table next to them.

"I don't know about you, but I don't think this will be a late night for me. All that thinking today combined with the fresh air has me so relaxed," Allie said. She sighed contentedly, munching on a cracker loaded with hummus.

"Same here," he said casually. The flames from the fire cast a warm glow over her features, creating shadows and light, highlighting her delicate beauty. "I will need some help from you in the morning hitching up the boat, then we'll load our stuff in the car and drop the boat off on our way out of town. I figure if we get off by noon, that will give us time to decompress before our Monday morning routine begins." He glanced at Allie with an enigmatic expression.

"Zane…" "Allie…" They both spoke at the same time.

"You go first," Allie commanded.

"No, you."

"Well, I'm not sure if I can express how I'm feeling right now, but I'll give it a try," she said, wringing her hands. "First, your generosity is above and beyond. Thank you for the amazing hospitality this weekend. Secondly, I know how hard this weekend has been, and your self-restraint has been impressive. You could have just said to hell with it and not worried about the consequences or damage, but you didn't. You thought about me, you cared about my wellbeing. That shows an unselfishness, and I want you to know that I noticed, and it was truly appreciated."

She looked down and then back up again, meeting his deep blue eyes.

"However, I must admit that if it had been up to me, I probably would've thrown caution to the winds, damn the consequences, and maybe later regretted it. I'm so glad not to be leaving the weekend with a regret hangover," she said with a shy smile. "You're really an extraordinary man, Zane Dunn."

"What were you going to say?" she asked.

Her sweet smile and admiration were his undoing. His voice husky with emotion, he said with difficulty, "Oh, Allie, you have no idea. I'm in heaven and hell at the same time. Exquisite torture." He shook his head. Taking her hand in his, he once again turned her hand up and began stroking her palm with his thumb, raising havoc with her nervous system.

"I'm not used to this confusion and self-doubt," he said. "I'm used to being in control of my emotions. I'm used to taking what I want. You've gotten under my skin like no one ever has. I ask myself 'What does this mean?' and I have no answers. I say to myself, 'Just one kiss. That's all. Just one. How can one kiss hurt anyone?' But I know it will only leave me longing for more …."

"But I have to have just one, Allie, God help me, just one." He leaned down to touch her full soft lips with his own.

At first, it was almost a hovering, barely touching,

skin grazing skin. She could feel his warm breath against her lips. She felt an immediate response in her core, a pulsating awareness that cried out for more contact. His lips pressed more, gently exploring. Her lips parted slightly, and he groaned. She felt his warm tongue tenderly explore hers. Not demanding, just inviting.

His soft tongue moved slowly in and out, dancing in an erotic rhythm. She parted her lips wider and he went deeper. She then thrust her tongue eagerly between his lips. Their tongues exploring one another until he gently began to suck on hers, drawing it in. She was lost in a swirl of eroticism.

Breathing heavily, Zane carefully pulled his head back, ending the kiss. Taking one look at her bemused expression, he was lost. Dipping his head, he went back for another taste of her. He buried his fingers in her luxuriously thick hair, holding her there to plunder. This time, the kiss was less gentle, and one borne of desperation. He drank of her. Tilting her head further back he kissed her exposed throat, her skin soft and smelling of floral and spice. He nuzzled her neck and moved behind her ear, whispering endearments while planting soft kisses.

Zane's breath was ragged, "Allie, I want you so badly. You have no idea what you do to me. I'm almost out of my mind with longing." He pulled her onto his lap, cradling her like a precious gift. His hand reached up under her camisole and he cupped and massaged her full, swollen breast, circling her sensitive nipple with his thumb.

"Oh my God, Zane," she said. Her hands ran through

his thick curling hair as she pulled him closer against her. "More please." She was lost. She wanted him with a primal lust that was completely foreign to her.

He pulled his hand from beneath her clothing and buried his nose in her hair, savoring her feminine scent.

"Don't stop," she pleaded. She could feel his erection against her buttocks, large and hard, yet he made no move to go any further. With his finger he lifted her chin and leaned down and gently kissed her moist lips.

"That put the kibosh on the hot tub for tonight," he said dryly. "Allie, I suggest you head on to bed before this gets any more complicated."

Still aroused, she was momentarily confused by his sudden change of direction, "But, Zane?"

"Go to bed now, Allie. Please!" It took all his willpower to send her off to bed. It was not what he wanted at all. He wanted to feel her naked flesh against his own. He wanted to please her until she was writhing in his arms with reckless abandon. However, he didn't want to take advantage of this volatile situation and have Allie, or himself for that matter, regret it later.

Embarrassed, Allie rose from his lap and hurried inside the house and to her bedroom. Closing the door, she leaned her back against it and slid all the way to the floor, drawing her knees to her chest, arms wrapped around them. Dropping her head, she quietly cried.

CHAPTER 8

After an impossibly restless night, Allie gave up on sleeping and jumped into the shower. Letting the hot water and strong jets stream across her shoulders soothed her. Today was a new day. She was going to forget all about last night's episode and consider it an aberration. She could effectively compartmentalize that love scene and place it in a very secure box with duct tape. The newly awakened arousal would have to be tamped back down. She would be okay. Mind over matter. Dreading that she had to face Zane again, she would hold her chin up and keep her traitorous body in check.

Zane was nowhere to be found and relief flooded her. There was fresh coffee brewed, so she grabbed a mug and filled it, leaving plenty of room for her half-and-half. She grabbed a stool and saddled up to the bar. Sipping the steaming beverage with satisfaction, she was so lost in thought that Zane startled her with his entrance.

"I see you found the coffee."

She jumped at the sound of his voice.

"Yes. Thank you," she said coolly.

"I have the car backed down to the dock, ready to be hitched to the boat with your help. No rush, but I thought we could just pick up some fast-food breakfast sandwiches and eat them on the road, if you don't mind?" he said, making another attempt to engage Allie.

"Yes, I'm fine with that. The sooner we get on the road the better, as far as I'm concerned," she said. She kept her head down and avoided looking at Zane.

"Is your luggage packed up yet? I can go ahead and haul it out after we hitch up the boat...that is, if it's ready to go," Zane said.

"Yep. Ready."

"I'll meet you outside by the dock." Trying to make eye contact, he said, "Allie?" He reached out to touch her arm, she jerked away like she had been burnt.

"Don't touch me, Zane."

"Allie, can we...." He was interrupted.

"No, Zane, we can't."

He turned abruptly and said, "Have it your way then. I'll see you at the dock."

"You're the boss," she said smartly.

"Real nice, Allie," he said, shutting the door with a little more force than was necessary.

The trip home seemed to take forever. Zane was grim faced and silent, obviously still angry with her about her earlier outburst. In fairness to him, Allie did admit that he had been the one to stop it from going any further the night before, and it was the right call. At least she could give him credit for that.

She felt embarrassed by her reckless abandon with Zane. It was out of character for her. She had only given herself completely to one other man, her ex-husband. They had both been virgins, so she wasn't that experienced. She was out of her league here. She believed in communication and conflict resolution, so withholding herself made her uncomfortable. However, she also didn't have the strength or clarity to work it out now, so she stayed silent.

"Are you comfortable driving straight through without stopping for lunch today?" Zane inquired stiffly.

His detachment and formality were like a knife in Allie's heart, and she knew she had hurt his feelings, but she also knew she had to let it ride for now. "Not only comfortable, I prefer it," she said with equal reserve.

"We can stop for a bathroom break at some point down the road."

"Fine," she said.

He did not respond this time, only pressed down on the accelerator as she watched the speedometer jump well above the speed limit. She noticed that his hands seemed to be gripping the wheel a little tighter than on Friday. Not quite as relaxed, and it gave Allie some small sense of satisfaction that she wasn't the only one who was miserable.

Several hours later, they turned down her lane and she was glad that the tense ride was over. The second the car stopped, she unlatched her seatbelt and jumped out of the vehicle. Going around to the trunk, she impatiently waited for Zane to pop the hatch so she could grab her bag. She practically ran to the house while pulling her suitcase behind; she fumbled for her keys, successfully pulling them out of her coat pocket just as she reached the door.

Zane came up behind her and tried to take the keys from her tight grip, but she held on. "I've got this."

"I'm sure you do, Allie, but please allow me." She reluctantly released her grip rather than engaging in a silly tug of war and he slipped the key in the lock and opened the door.

Pulling her bag inside, she set it beside the door and called out for Kit Kat in a singsong voice.

"Kit, Mama's home." No response. Worried, she began to look around. "This is so unlike her. Normally she is waiting by the door to greet me."

Zane had followed her inside, and he, too, began to call out for her. "Here, kitty-kitty." Nothing.

As Allie got further into the house, she felt a breeze coming from the kitchen. Her French door stood ajar, letting in the cool air.

"Oh no, I hope Kit Kat didn't get outside." That was her first thought, quickly followed by her second: Why was her door ajar?

Just then, Zane called from the living room, "Here she is." Carrying her in his arms, he stopped short of the open door. "She was hiding under the chair," he said.

"This door was open, and I know I didn't leave it that way. I triple-checked everything before I left the house."

"Maybe your nieces forgot to close it when they fed Kit?" he wondered aloud.

"I'm sure that's it," she agreed. "They are only ten years old, after all. Usually my sister-in-law follows behind them, but maybe she stayed in the car this time."

"If you don't mind, I'll take a look around the rest of the house to make sure it's secure," he said.

"I'd really appreciate that. It's so strange for Kit to be hiding under a chair. She's such an outgoing cat."

"I'll be right back." He left to search for anything else that might be out of place or unusual. Upstairs, nothing appeared disturbed in the first of three bedrooms. Her artistic touch was everywhere. As with the downstairs, she had put a lot of effort in creating a beautiful space, with each room having its own unique flare.

Reassured that there was nothing out of sorts in the first or second rooms, he entered the larger master suite and did a walkthrough. Curious to know more about Allie, he took his time studying her dresser top and bookshelves for clues into her inner world. Fancy perfume bottles, antique jewel boxes, a loaded earring stand draped with sparkling earrings and necklaces, all created an alluring picture of femininity. There was a framed photograph of her sitting on a horse, another posing with two young girls, and another of her with two other women with an ocean in the background, one of whom he suspected was her mother, since the resemblance was obvious.

He found that the bathroom equally embodied the feminine. Makeup mirror, lotions, fancy towels on the rack, and a woman's scent lingered, even though she had been away for two days. Finding nothing amiss, he returned downstairs to Allie, who was fiddling with the French door latch as he came up beside her.

"I think I discovered the problem. This latch is a little wonky. They probably just didn't secure it when they left." She smiled with relief. "Everything clear upstairs?"

"Yes, it appears to be in order." He stooped to take a closer look at the door latch, agreeing with her assessment.

"Well, Allie, it has been an interesting weekend to say the least." He looked deep into her eyes.

"Yes," she said. "Thanks for checking out the house. Thanks for everything." She followed him to the front door, using every ounce of her willpower not to reach out and ask him to stay, to kiss her, to say to hell with restraint, but she managed to contain her churning emotions.

He stood awkwardly, like he wanted to say more but then decided against it. "Take care, Allie. I will see you at the office." And, like that, he was gone.

Allie hugged herself, trying to ignore the empty feeling inside. "Kit Kat, let's think about dinner." Her appetite was nonexistent, but she knew she had to go through the motions. With Kit seemingly back to her old self, weaving in and out around Allie's legs, she grabbed a can of cat food off the shelf, and scooped a large portion into the cat's dish.

She threw some seasoning and extra cheese on a frozen pizza then placed it in the oven. Back to her old standby. Remembering she still had some bagged lettuce mix, she decided to add a tossed salad to the menu. Feeling despondent, Allie decided to light a fire in the fireplace. After dinner she would snuggle in with a good book. Maybe that would help pick up her spirits.

Nothing like a good novel, a cat on your lap, and a warm comforting fire to cure what ails you. She would phone her mom later to let her know she was home safe and sound. Tomorrow she would check in with Casey to get a much-needed pep talk with the best listening ear she knew.

~

*Z*ane drummed his fingers as he waited impatiently for the garage door to open. He slipped into the first stall of his four-car garage; parking next to the Alfa Romeo Spider convertible. He turned off the engine but did not immediately get out.

He was frustrated, to say the least. And angry with himself for letting temptation steer him in such a dangerous direction with Allie. He never mixed business with pleasure. He liked to keep the lines clear between his personal life and his professional one. He had messed up royally this time. He had no excuse, but if he were to allow one, it would be that his work with her over the last few months had allowed him to get to know and respect her without the complications of romantic pressures.

He had observed her at the office and knew her to be well liked by all the staff. She was warm and friendly with everyone. She was always upbeat and, like himself, seemed to keep her personal life where it belonged, out of the office. She was also an asset to the law firm. She had caught on to the job very quickly. She was smart, had great critical thinking ability, and an excellent work ethic. The last thing he wanted was to blow it and lose the best paralegal he had ever hired because of his sexual desire for her.

Deep down, he admitted it was more than just a casual attraction. He also knew he would have to contain this for both himself and Allie, for the sake of the office and their careers. Sighing with grim determination, he got out of the car and unloaded the luggage and leftover groceries. Spying the wine poking out of the bag brought back images of the previous night in vivid detail. Remembering her swollen lips, the feel of her soft, full breasts pressed against him, her complete abandon, all he wanted was to jump back into the car and race over to Allie's house to finish what they had started.

CHAPTER 9

The following day, Allie decided to call in sick. She needed to give herself a day to recuperate. She certainly had plenty to catch up on after her weekend away. They would just have to do without her. She felt a pang of guilt but quickly squashed it down. She had earned a day off since she had put in some time on the case over the weekend. If she was avoiding the inevitable for a day, she could forgive herself. She would make up for it on Tuesday. After calling the office and leaving a voicemail, she felt much better. Tomorrow would be soon enough to come face-to-face with Zane. *Give me strength.*

Shortly after nine her phone rang, and it was her colleague on the other end.

"OMG," Annika said without preamble. "What the heck happened over the weekend? Our esteemed boss is walking around the office like a bear with a thorn in his paw. He can be intense at the best of times, but we are all tiptoeing around him, hoping not to draw any attention to ourselves. His mood seemed to move from bad to worse after he heard that you'd called in sick."

With her usual discretion, Allie told her friend she needed a day of rest after the busy work weekend. "I need to catch up on things around the house like laundry, cleaning, paying bills, checking in on Mel," she ticked off her list.

Annika, sounding dubious, said, "Please just make sure you're back here tomorrow or there might not be an office to return to." She hmphed and added, "I can't wait to hear all about your work weekend at the lake. I would've liked to have been a fly on the wall, for sure. I'd better get off the phone before the boss comes out from his lair. See you tomorrow."

Hanging up the phone with a smile at her friend's curiosity, Allie realized she would have to come up with a good story for Annika. The last thing she or Zane needed was office gossip putting the two of them together in a romantic light. She was glad she was creative.

Dialing Casey's number, she waited for her friend to pick up. "Hello," Casey said.

Relief flooded Allie, just hearing her friend's voice on the other end. "Casey, I'm in trouble. Do you have a few minutes to talk?" she asked.

"Of course. I'm all ears," she said, then, hearing the panic in her friend's tone, she said, "I'm assuming the weekend didn't go too well?"

"I'm a mess, quite frankly. I'm in way over my head and I desperately need your advice," she said. "Things started out a little awkwardly, but we got over that hump and had a very pleasant trip to the lake. I will admit to my attraction. Zane out of his professional mode is a force of nature. I'm not kidding. He looked like a Greek god, and he was all funny and charming and relaxed." The words tumbled out of Allie in a torrent. "I tried to resist but things got really heated the second night, and I might have gone further than I would have liked, and he is my boss and I have the biggest crush and, *oh, Casey*, what am I going to *do*?" she wailed.

"You're going to quit beating up on yourself for starters. You are both consenting adults the last time I checked. Have you looked at yourself in the mirror lately? How could anyone resist you, and he must have had a clue going into this trip that there would be temptation."

"Yes, well he did admit to having a slight attraction going into the weekend, but he said he didn't realize how strong it was until we were spending this time outside of work together. He even apologized, saying he would never want to take advantage of his position as my boss."

"I call BS," Casey said. "This guy is rich, successful, gorgeous, powerful, and sexy as all get-out from the newspaper photos and from your descriptions. He would have to know the impact he has on women. Don't take this all on yourself. So, how far did it go?"

"Well, let's just say I've never experienced that level of desire in my life. I lost myself Casey. I didn't want him to stop." Blushing at the memory, she continued, "The worst part is, he's the one who put on the brakes and basically sent me to bed like a child. I have never felt more embarrassed in my life."

"Hey, why should you be embarrassed?" Her friend pointed out, "There's nothing wrong with being a sexually alive woman who knows how to enjoy and love her body and her sensuality. It's a gift."

"Intellectually I know all of that, but emotionally I have never been as completely carried away as I was with Zane. His kisses were divine. His touch..." Allie continued, "The passion between us was off the charts. I would have—without question—gone to bed with him if he hadn't stopped it from happening."

"I'm totally jealous. What are you complaining about? I think you should be celebrating. It's about time you came back to life," her friend said cheerfully.

Allie smiled at Casey's no-nonsense perspective. "Maybe you're right, and I'm putting too much importance on our brief interlude. I was so embarrassed that the following morning I completely blew him off when he tried to reach out to me. I was quite rude, actually."

"You were just having a moment," Casey said.

"I know I hurt his feelings, but I just—if we are going to continue to work together, I have to put the genie back in the box. This thing, whatever this *thing* is, feels dangerously hot...someone is going to get burnt, and chances are it'll be me." Allie let out a huge sigh, "Thank you, Casey, I feel better already."

"For what? I didn't tell you anything you didn't already know."

"You always say just the right thing to get me out of my irrational self and back to reality. I don't know how I'd get through life without you."

"That's what friends are for, and you've done the same for me a thousand times or so. It goes both ways." Casey said earnestly.

"I actually called in sick today. You know that is totally not me. How am I going to handle going back to work tomorrow?"

"You're going to dress carefully in the morning so that you feel your absolute best—mascara, gloss, hair, the works. Then you're going to remember what I'm about to say to you: You are one of the smartest, funniest, most compassionate, loving, beautiful—as in drop-dead-gorgeous—women I have ever met. Zane Dunn was blessed by the gods when he was lucky enough to land you as his assistant. He knows it, I know it, and you need to know it. He does not have all the power here. Get in touch with your inner goddess and embrace her. Allie, eventually you're going to need to come out of your shell. Your ex-husband never deserved you. He was a loser from day one. His infidelity had nothing to do with you and your desirability and everything to do with him being a misogynistic jerk," she said frankly.

Laughing, Allie felt like a thousand pounds had been lifted from her shoulders. "I love you so much, Case."

"I love you too. Now, take the day to regroup and walk into the office tomorrow morning like you own the joint," she said firmly.

Thrusting her fist in the air she said, "Okay, girls' rule! I'll do it for all the working women of the world. Onward to empowerment."

"I have full confidence in you. Keep me posted," Casey said.

"As if I have a choice," Allie said. "Bye."

"You got that right. Bye."

After her talk with Casey, she headed out the door to enjoy some much-needed barn time. Earlier, she had called Laura to volunteer to do the stalls today since she had missed out over the weekend. Laura, who knew Allie well, was a little surprised to hear that her friend was playing hooky from work, but she was glad to have the help and said so.

"That is great news. I have to take Jake's mom to a doctor appointment this afternoon, so that'll help a lot," Laura said. "We are so looking forward to Thanksgiving. Let me know when it gets closer if there's anything else I can bring besides the pies."

"Not that I can think of at the moment, but I'll let you know," Allie said.

CHAPTER 10

Tuesday arrived. With a pit in her stomach but fortified by her conversation with Casey and her killer outfit, Allie stepped out of the elevator into the office. She'd no sooner sat down when Annika came over to her desk and said, "Zane wants to see you as soon as you get in." Allie's stomach somersaulted.

"Thanks Annika. I'll go right in."

"Good luck," Annika said. She scrutinized her friend's face, looking for clues.

"Ha. Don't be silly, Annika. I've been working with Zane for months; he doesn't scare me." Trying to redirect her friend's thoughts, she asked, "Can you do lunch today?"

"Sorry, I have plans, but how about later in the week?"

"Sold." Allie rose from her desk and made her way to Zane's office.

Knocking lightly, she cracked the door, and stuck her head in. "You wanted to see me?"

Zane was on the phone. He held up one finger and motioned her inside. Taking a seat, she fiddled with her bracelets while waiting for his conversation to end.

He studied her while listening to the person on the other end of the phone. Her eyes were lowered, so she didn't see the haunted look in his eyes. Her slim-fitting navy slacks and cream silky V-neck blouse with pearl buttons flattered her slim yet curvy figure. *Professional, yet on her, somehow sexy.* The tortoiseshell reading glasses perched atop her nose gave her the quintessential sexy librarian look and were unintentionally seductive. Her hair was loose and flowed freely around her shoulders. He had missed her.

"I understand, but I need any new discoveries on my desk by noon or I will take it up with the judge," Zane said. His commanding voice brooked no argument. He was in his element. Strong, brilliant, self-assured, nobody's fool. "No, you have already had two weeks to get that information to my office and have failed to do so. By noon today, no later, and that's final." He hung up and rubbed his hands over his face before raking them through his hair.

"Are you feeling better today, Allie? I wouldn't want you to push yourself too soon." His sarcasm was not lost on her, as his dubious expression belied the concern of his words.

"Yes, thank you. Much better Mr. Dunn. You wanted to see me?" Two can play that game, as she made sure to wear her most innocent expression.

"Yes. Dammit, Allie," he practically growled, "don't you think we're way beyond 'Mr. Dunn' at this point?"

"No," she replied stubbornly. "Unless something has happened that I'm unaware of, you're still my boss and I'm still your employee, *and* I'm on the clock." She looked at him defiantly, almost daring him to say more.

"Whatever," he said in exasperation. "There has been some new discovery in the Havers case that the prosecution has been withholding from us. Apparently, one of our witnesses has flipped for the prosecution. I have no idea what that means for our case, but I am expecting the information to be delivered by noon today. We will have to go over this new evidence immediately in order to prepare our response. Please look for it and buzz me the minute it arrives."

All business now, the dancer, cook, captain, and lover had been replaced with the consummate attorney. Allie felt a pang of loss but knew she was responsible for his withdrawal.

"I think it might be a good idea to get Will Havers on the phone after we go through the discovery together. Could you line that up for maybe around three o'clock this afternoon?"

This, Allie knew how to deal with. "I'll get right on it," she said, all business herself. "Anything else?"

Zane stared at her with an intensity that made his blue eyes feel like lasers burning through her protective layers. Chin tilted up; she met his gaze with equal determination. He looked away first.

"Nothing for now. Alright, Allie, I'll see you in a little while." He leaned back in his leather chair and watched her leave his office, he called out as she reached the door, "I'll have our lunch delivered, so we can work right on through."

"Sounds like a plan. I'll let you know when the courier arrives."

"Thank you, Allie," he said. Beyond frustrated by her aloofness, he wondered if this was going to be the new normal. Not if he had anything to say about it.

"Just doing my job, *sir*," she said. She felt a slight pang of guilt for getting one more dig in before closing the door behind her.

After the courier delivered the documents, Allie stood behind Zane, leaning over his shoulder to study the legal papers. "Well, I just don't believe the witness's statement here. I interviewed him several times because he was one of Will's full-time employees. This information was never stated until now. This is a completely new version of events. I think someone has gotten to him Zane. He was forced to recant," Allie said with concern.

"You may be right." Her light floral scent tantalized him, so he got up from his desk and paced around the room. "His previous testimony corroborated everything Will said. This could be a big problem. As long as we can get his previous declaration entered into the trial for the jury to hear, it may cancel this version out." He sighed heavily. "We did not need this complication, that's for sure."

Moments later, Zane's intercom buzzed, and Stella, Zane's personal receptionist, said, "Mr. Dunn, Mr. Fletcher is here again. He insists on talking to you. What should I do?" she asked.

With an exasperated sigh, he responded, "Bring him on back. I'll deal with him."

"Thank you, Mr. Dunn," Stella said with relief.

Practically everyone in the firm was familiar with the loud and obnoxious Mr. Fletcher. Smith, Dunn, Rogers, and Browne had represented him in a case where the judgment had gone for the plaintiff. He could not accept the outcome and made regular visits to the firm to bully and complain about his lack of representation. In hindsight, they wished they hadn't taken the case, but that didn't do them any good now.

There was a knock at the door and Allie opened it. She turned toward Zane and asked, "Should I step out, Mr. Dunn?"

"No, I would prefer that you stay, if you don't mind."

"Of course." She took a seat.

A short, stout man with a bulbous nose and a ruddy red complexion, obviously prone to rosacea, pushed his way past Stella and stood threateningly in front of Zane's desk. Pointing and shaking his finger, he began hurling insults at Zane. "You couldn't defend even if you were playing defensive guard in a peewee football league. You are a joke, and I intend to sue this firm for every penny I can get." He was becoming increasingly red with every word uttered. His puffy round face looked like it was ready to explode. Allie thought he could even stroke out if he didn't calm down.

Allie spoke soothingly, "Now, Mr. Fletcher, maybe you should calm down and have a seat."

"Don't *you* tell *me* to calm down, missy. I am not going to calm down until this firm admits to misrepresenting me. This S.O.B. here. Mr. Fancy Pants, drives around in his fancy cars, getting rich off poor folks like me. Laughing all the way to the bank." Changing his mind about sitting, since he was breathless from the exertion, he jerked the chair toward him and plopped down, passing gas rather loudly as he sat.

Allie looked over at Zane, suppressing her laughter, her eyes alight with merriment. His expression remained impassive, but she could see annoyance mixed with slight amusement in his eyes.

"Well now, Mr. Fletcher, there is no need for the insults. We have had this discussion before, and, as I stated previously, the prosecutor had ample evidence supporting the plaintiff's accusations. Even so, we thought we had a strong defense case until we were blindsided by the new evidence that came out at trial. We objected to the undisclosed discovery, but it was overruled. Had you leveled with us to begin with, we would not have been caught by surprise and could have been prepared to rebut their claim. Since they found witnesses at the last minute, whose testimony placed you outside of Mrs. Dorsey's window, peeking in and trying to enter, it was very difficult to discredit two different accounts of the same action by you. As it is, we reduced your bill by half and agreed to a very fair payment plan." Zane spoke quietly but in a deadly calm tone, obviously making a concerted effort to keep his cool.

When Mr. Fletcher leaned back, he not only exposed a portion of his ample white belly but also that his fly was gaping open, displaying his white underwear. When Allie saw this, she snorted with laughter then attempted to disguise it by covering her mouth and faking a sneeze.

Zane had to look away for a moment to visibly compose himself. "Mr. Fletcher is there anything that would satisfy you, short of a not-guilty verdict?"

"Well, seeing as I am now a registered sex offender, I think I've paid my dues. I may be willing to stop pursuing a case against your firm if you were to drop my bill in the trash." He crossed his arms and sneered at Zane defiantly.

"You know, I may agree to forget about your balance if you promise to never step foot in this law firm again, never call this firm again, and never approach me or my staff anywhere ever again. Do we have an agreement?" Zane said with authority.

"You know I am a reasonable man." Fletcher preened. "I promise, but I don't trust any of you lawyers, so I want it in writing," he said. Proud of himself for thinking of it.

"I will get my secretary to write that up immediately. Now, get the hell out of my office," Zane said. He stood to emphasize his point.

"Hey, no hard feelings, Mr. Dunn, no need to get all huffy." Like most bullies when met with someone more powerful, he completely collapsed into a sniveling coward.

The minute the door closed behind the waddling Mr. Fletcher; Allie could not contain herself any longer. She took one look at Zane and they both erupted in laughter. Allie noticed with relief that any tension that had been between them before was now gone. They were a team again, on the same side.

"On that note," Zane said, "what could possibly be the encore?"

Visualizing Mr. Fletcher returning in all his glory for the final bow was her undoing. She doubled over in another fit of laughter. "Oh my God, I can't breathe!" She gasped. Suddenly, she looked up and caught Zane staring at her with a raw hunger in his eyes and she abruptly stilled. The moment stretched on for what felt like minutes but was in reality only seconds.

"Allie, I can't tell you how good it feels to have you back again," he said.

"I feel the same way, Zane. I don't want there to be a distance between us. I love working here at this firm and with you. This is so much more than just a job for me. We're a team, you and me, functioning like a well-oiled machine. I don't want to jeopardize that."

"I would be lying to you if I said I'm content with just a working friendship now, but I'll do my best to accept it," Zane said. "It's probably the wisest course."

CHAPTER 11

The next several weeks flew by for Allie, with no suspicious activity or calls. They checked in frequently with Will and were reassured that things appeared quiet for the moment. In the meantime, the firm had hired a P.I. named Darcy Morgan, whom they had used several times in the past. She was an ex-cop who, deciding that the private sector was more to her liking, had hung up her badge to go into business for herself. It had paid off. She was feisty and fearless and relentless in her pursuit of information. Like a bloodhound, she was innately born to sniff out and follow the scent.

Late one afternoon, Allie and Zane were holed up in his office when Zane got up and began pacing. "I'm not just concerned for Will and his family, Allie. I'm worried about you as well. Even though nothing more has happened I'd feel a hell of a lot more comfortable if you weren't living alone out in the middle of nowhere."

He stopped pacing and was now perched on the edge of his desk inches from Allie. His brows drew together, and his jaw clenched.

"Zane, I'm fine. I took a self-defense class and I now carry pepper spray. Quit worrying."

"I'm going to give you one of my guns and have Darcy teach you how to use it."

"I'm on board for that. Then will you quit worrying?"

"Probably not, but it will help. I care about you." His eyes burned with emotion as he leaned closer. "I could never forgive myself if something happened to you."

The air in the room suddenly crackled with sexual tension. Allie drew her lower lip between her teeth. Like a moth to the flame she couldn't look away as his eyes blazed with desire. He reached for her hand pulling her from her seat into his arms. He held her between his legs hugging her tightly to his chest. Nuzzling her neck, he whispered, "I want you Allie. I've tried fighting it... you want it too; tell me you don't want it as bad as I do."

She couldn't.

Zane looked into her lust-filled eyes and was lost. He tilted her head back and kissed the hollow of her throat. She moaned. Standing, he reversed positions, lifting her easily onto his desk, he stood between her legs. Her thighs felt soft and creamy as he pushed her skirt up around her hips. He lifted her knees and spread them wide as he rubbed his growing erection against her dainty underwear. He covered her mouth with his, thrusting his tongue deep inside.

She was lost, his scent of cedar and soap, his bulging penis pressed against her sweet spot, his hands now moving to cup her breasts were more than she could resist.

"Yes, Zane please," she panted against his mouth. He rubbed his thumbs across her nipples as she arched her back to press against him. She buried her fingers in his thick hair.

Suddenly they heard a commotion outside the office followed by a knock. Zane quickly pulled Allie's skirt down and stepped away as she stood and put space between them. The door banged open and a stunningly beautiful woman with jet black hair and eyes that matched stormed in. Stella, trailing behind, apologized profusely. "I tried to stop her, Mr. Dunn. She wouldn't listen."

"Oh Stella, zip it," the dark beauty snapped.

She looked Allie up and down as if she were examining something distasteful. "Well, who have we here? Another one of your conquests?" Allie's bee stung lips and flushed cheeks weren't lost on her.

"Hello to you too, Helen. Allie, Helen. Helen, Allie," he said by way of introduction. "How can I help you?" Zane asked her, unruffled.

Looking at Allie she said, "Can we please have a moment alone?" Her condescending tone making it more of a demand than a request.

"Allie, I'm sorry that Helen appears to have given up on all attempts at civility, but would you mind stepping out of the office and giving us a few minutes alone? I'm sure whatever she has to say won't take long."

"Of course," Allie said, awkwardly moving to the door, wanting to put as much distance between her and Medusa as quickly as possible.

As she stood, she felt like her skin was being peeled off by the intensity of the woman's glare. "She is a pretty one, I will give you that. Then again, you always did have excellent taste in everything, didn't you my love? After all, you did pick me," Helen said, laughing at her own wit.

Allie hurried out of the office, quietly closing the door behind her. So, this was the infamous Helen. Allie could tell that Helen had quickly sized up the situation and jumped to the correct conclusion. All she could think was, poor Zane. No wonder he had lost faith in women.

Allie knew Helen was also an attorney with a reputation for being merciless, in and out of the courtroom. She was also aware that she was no match for this creature and hoped to never get in her bad graces. But *wow*, she might possibly be the most beautiful woman Allie had ever laid eyes on. She would love to be a fly on the wall in there right about now. Zane was quite a powerhouse himself and based on Helen's entry, she would bet that sparks were sure to fly. She would also lay odds that Helen was the type that thrived on verbal sparring.

Allie walked over to Stella's desk, and it was obvious that she was still upset. "Oh, that woman," Stella exclaimed. "The nerve of her, storming in here and pushing her way past me. I'm so sorry Allie. She is the most arrogant and rude person I have ever known. Thank God they divorced. I was hoping to never have to deal with her again, but I guess I'm not going to be that lucky."

"Don't worry about it, Stella. There wasn't a thing you could have done to stop her. It must have been

pretty hard working here while they were still married."
She normally didn't engage in gossip, but her curiosity
was getting the better of her.

"You have no idea. I threatened to quit multiple
times, but the partners calmed me down and convinced
me to stay each time. At least she never worked for this
firm. I couldn't have handled that. She is the closest
thing to evil that I have had the displeasure of crossing
paths with."

"I am sure her beauty captivates most mortal men,"
Allie commented.

"Yes, like a black widow," Stella said, finally smiling
conspiratorially.

Allie walked behind Stella's desk and bent down to
give her a big hug. "You are the greatest, Stella. This
office couldn't function without you. I hope you know
that. Maybe we should get you a taser for the next time
she comes barging in," Allie said.

"I just hope there aren't too many 'next times,'" she
replied.

❧

"So, to what do I owe this dubious pleasure?"
Zane asked.

"Be nice, Zane. You know I still adore you. I don't
understand why we can't have another go at it," Helen
said, seeming honestly bewildered.

"Ha, really Helen? You can say that after your ruthless attempts to destroy me financially and otherwise?"
He shook his head incredulously.

"Zane, it's only money. You said that yourself. There

is no one out there like you. You are my equal. My alpha male. I need you," she said, complaining like a petulant child who's been denied a toy.

"You should have thought of that when you were banging your law partner. It would have saved a lot of heartbreak," Zane said.

Walking around the desk, she came up behind Zane and leaned down, whispering seductively in his ear, "Baby, I know I broke your heart, but I've changed. I've come to my senses now. I was momentarily blinded by lust. I plead temporary insanity. Totally stupid, I know that now. Surely you can understand, can't you?" Helen pleaded.

"Helen let's cut to the chase here. What are you really after?"

"Ouch, that hurts. Why would you think I'm after something? I was just in the neighborhood and wanted to stop in and see your gorgeous face. I miss you. Is that too much to expect after all of our history together?"

"Pardon me if I'm a little jaded here, but in my experience, you don't do anything that isn't calculated. Now, let me repeat my question: What are you doing here?"

"Well, if you must know, I have a bit of a dilemma. My house is under renovation, and I just can't handle the disruption another minute. I was hoping you'd be generous enough to let me use our lake house temporarily. Only for a month or two," she said. Smiling slyly, she added, "You can still come on the weekends and stay with me. Like old times." Helen began kneading his tense muscles. "Darling, your shoulders are so tight. I know what I could do to relieve some of that built-up tension." She leaned down and put her lips seductively against his ear. "We were always so good in bed together. Two wild animals mating," she whispered, as she put the tip of her tongue in his ear.

"Helen, cut it out," he said, jerking his head away and brushing at his ear. "First of all, it is not 'our' lake house, it is mine. Secondly, *if* I were to let you use it temporarily, and that is a big if, I would not be sharing it with you. That ship has sailed, and you know it. If you don't, you are more delusional than I thought. You burned your bridges to the ground with a vengeance," Zane said getting more perturbed as he spoke.

Pouting, Helen said, "I'm sorry you feel that way. We were good together at one point. I think we could have that again if you would give it a chance."

"Not going to happen, Helen. Just leave it at that. I'm not getting into it with you again. We've been over this a million times, and my answer hasn't changed. It's over. Now, I'll consider letting you use the lake house, but I need to think about it for a few days. I'll get back to you."

She looked at him calculatingly, "Does this indecision have anything to do with that beautiful blonde who looked like she'd just been fucked?" she asked cruelly.

His jaw clenched, "Leave Allie out of it."

"Oh, did I hit a nerve? I see I'm on to something." She smiled cynically. "You will never learn will you, Zane?"

"And what would it be that I am not learning?" he asked curiously, not able to resist the bait.

"Women can't be trusted. She might come off all sweet and innocent now, but once she has you, poof, the sweet innocent is gone. How can you ever be certain she is not after your money and power? I mean come on, a story as old as time, beautiful woman seducing her rich billionaire boss." Helen laughed wickedly. Seeing the doubt in Zane's eyes, she knew she'd hit her target. Satisfied, she offered to call him in several days to see what his answer would be.

"Don't bother calling me, Helen. I'll be in touch," Zane said, escorting her to the door.

When he opened the door, Helen surreptitiously glanced to see if Allie was within viewing range and satisfied that she was, put her arms around Zane's neck, pulling his head down for a light kiss on the lips. He quickly disentangled her arms from around him and said sternly, "Goodbye, Helen."

"Be good darling. I'll wait to hear from you then." And she confidently marched out of the office.

The air felt like it had been sucked out of the room. Zane went back into his office and closed the door. Allie, not sure what to do, opted to wait for his summons. He looked troubled as he shut the door. The summons never came.

Zane stayed sequestered for the remainder of the day. Allie left at five o'clock for the first time in weeks, filled with doubt. She wondered if he was now regretting their brief sexual transgression. She wondered if he still had feelings for Helen. She felt bad for Zane and wanted to reach out but knew that there was nothing she could say. She felt jealous but knew Helen had been trying to mark her territory and was doing it without Zane's consent. He would have to work through it himself. Helen made her feel oddly grateful that her ex was only a cheating jerk and that she'd never had to deal with him again after their divorce was finalized.

The following day work returned to normal. Whatever demons Zane had battled must have been slain. They picked up where they had left off before their intimate interlude.

"I hope we don't have any more surprise visitors today," Allie said.

He nodded his head and said, "Yes, we can agree on that. Yesterday totally threw me off my game, but I'm back on track today. Thanks for your understanding."

Allie waited for him to say more but he dove straight into work. She shrugged it off and they were immediately back in sync like nothing had ever happened... almost...except it was impossible to deny the sexual tension in the room. But they both seemed determined to try.

CHAPTER 12

*F*inally, it was here—the Wednesday before Thanksgiving. Tomorrow was the big day. The law firm was closing at noon and not reopening until the following Monday to give its staff extra time off for the holiday. Allie was putting away the last of her files when Zane walked by her desk, on his way back from a meeting with his partners at the other end of their ninth-floor offices.

He stopped by to wish her a happy Thanksgiving. "Thank you, Zane. What are your big plans for turkey day?" she asked curiously.

"I have no plans. Couch, football, beer, I'm just a lonely bachelor. Don't you feel sorry for me?" He smiled at her warmly and she allowed herself a moment to stare. She loved the laugh lines around his eyes and the way the deep blue seemed to sparkle when he smiled.

Allie still marveled at the recent transformation in Zane. The man she had once considered aloof had decided to let her in. They had made an unspoken agreement to stay in the friend zone. Although still moody at times, he no longer held himself at arm's length, at least with her. The interlude in the office had been filed away. There was a real friendship blossoming and a mutual respect that she delighted in. They had returned to a comfortable rhythm in their work together. He had been in a noticeably better mood recently, igniting speculation around the office about the two of them, but Allie just ignored it. Let them think what they wanted. She didn't really care.

Allie knew Zane had no family living close by. She remembered that his mom lived in California and that his dad lived somewhere out West as well. She knew they'd divorced when Zane was in college. It made her sad to think of him home alone on the holiday, especially one that was about gatherings and sharing food with loved ones. "Hey, I have an idea," Allie said. "Why don't you come to my house for dinner? There will be fifteen of us, well now the count is sixteen, because I invited Darcy, so what's one more?"

"Darcy? As in Darcy Morgan?" His interest was piqued.

Allie felt a pang of jealousy, wondering if Zane could be interested in the P.I. She couldn't blame him. A stunning redhead with a million-watt personality would be attractive to just about anyone. "Yes, that Darcy. I invited her when she was giving me lessons at the shooting range."

"How's your aim?"

"I could hit the side of a barn now, I'm pretty sure. So, will you come?"

The corners of his eyes crinkled as he smiled at Allie. "Thank you for the invite."

"I would love to have you. You don't have to answer now. You can think about it and just drop in if you feel like it. Just bring yourself. Everyone is arriving around three o'clock, but we won't actually eat dinner until five." She smiled. "I really hope you make it. You'll love my family and friends. They're all great company and easy to get along with. Kind of like me," she winked saucily.

"I won't make any promises, but I'll see what I can do," he replied.

"Okay, I'm out of here. I've got a mile-long list of things I'd like to accomplish before one o'clock tomorrow. If I don't see you, have a nice holiday. Don't watch too much football and try to get in some relaxation. You work too hard."

"Thanks, Mom. Don't burn the gobbler."

"I'll do my best. Bye, Zane."

"Bye, Allie."

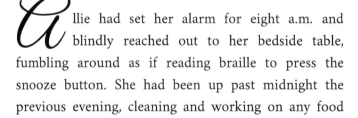

*A*llie had set her alarm for eight a.m. and blindly reached out to her bedside table, fumbling around as if reading braille to press the snooze button. She had been up past midnight the previous evening, cleaning and working on any food prep she could do in advance.

After three snooze cycles, she reluctantly crawled out of bed. Putting on her slippers and bathrobe, she ambled downstairs, followed by Kit Kat, to start her day. First, she fed Kit, then put on a pot of coffee. While waiting for the coffee to drip, she pulled on a jacket and went outside to fill her bird feeder. Or more accurately, her squirrel feeder. Throwing a handful of unsalted roasted peanuts, the waiting squirrels hungrily snatched two at a time to make sure they got their share.

She returned to the kitchen and plopped down on a stool at the counter island, going over her to-do list as she enjoyed her morning cup of java with her usual companion sitting at her feet staring up at her. "Kit, I am sure there will be plenty of turkey coming your way if you hang by the table tonight."

She needed to bring in some wood from outside for the fire. Most of the things on her list she had done the night before. The potatoes were already peeled, sitting in the fridge, carrots and brussels sprouts the same. She was pleased with the Thanksgiving center piece she had picked up from the florist earlier in the week. She had long tapered candles that she would light during their feast. Continuing down her list, checking things off as she went: tablecloth, Grandma's antique china hauled out of storage and washed, wine chilled, house clean. What remained could only be done closer to mealtime.

She glanced at her watch; she'd better jump in the shower. It was already nine thirty.

As she showered, her thoughts drifted to Zane. She wondered if he would show up today. If he did, it would be the first time they'd been together outside of the office since the lake house. She felt a little thrill of antic-ipation at the thought. As she lathered her breasts, she remembered how it felt to have his hands softly caressing them. *Nope, Allie, not going there.* She rinsed off and stepped out of the shower. Grabbing a big fluffy white towel, she dried off then threw on some old clothes while she worked on the turkey; later she would dress with more care for the party.

After getting the bird in the oven, Allie quickly ran upstairs to get dressed before her guests arrived. She chose a short gray pencil skirt that fit like a glove. The blouse she decided on was a pale peach silk with a V neckline that plunged daringly low, revealing the slight swell of her breasts and subtle glimpses of her peach bra. She wore the same dangly silver earrings and added a long silver chain with a medallion of a horse that nestled in the V between her breasts. She pulled on her favorite tall gray suede boots that came slightly above the knee. Dabbing a drop of perfume behind each ear, she looked at herself one last time in the full-length mirror. She had opted to pull her hair into a loose French braid to keep it out of the way while she was preparing the food. Tendrils were already escaping the confines of the clasp. Satisfied with her appearance, she went back downstairs to wait for her guests.

Casey and her clan were the first to arrive. Casey's husband Charlie and her brother Sam lugged in the food Casey had prepared while Casey's daughter Clare held tight to a leash with a bundle of energy at the other end. At Allie's suggestion, they had brought along Dugan, their shepherd mix. Kit Kat eyed Dugan disdainfully. He obviously had experience with felines because he observed her warily and avoided getting too close.

"You're a good boy, Dugan," Allie crooned. Dugan

barked his agreement, tail wagging vigorously. "You and Kit are going to get loads of treats today."

Darcy arrived at the same time as Allie's brother Mark and his family, with the Johnston gang bringing up the rear. Last to arrive was her mom with her date, Pete. Sarah sported a flattering new hairstyle. She practically glowed. It was apparent that she and Pete were in love.

There was a knock at the door, and Allie's breath caught in her throat. She hadn't realized that she'd been waiting. Sam opened the door and Zane stepped through the threshold as Allie went to greet him. His eyes quickly scanned the room until they lighted upon her, and she saw them darken with an inscrutable emotion. He looked a little unsure of himself as he handed a bouquet of fresh flowers to Allie. In his other hand, he held a bottle of wine. Staring at Allie, he gave a low whistle.

"Wow, Allie, you look beautiful!"

Blushing at his compliment, Allie said, "You don't look too shabby yourself, Mr. Dunn." She could barely contain her happiness at seeing him.

Sensing his awkwardness, she grabbed his hand and led him into the fray. He looked so sexy in his low-slung black Levi's, worn with a belt and black tee that hugged his super-fit body. She could hardly keep her hands off him. *Down, girl.*

"Hey, everyone, this is Zane," she announced to the group.

He quickly relaxed and fit right in with the crowd. The kids slipped out the kitchen door to play games in the back yard while the adults watched football and visited over the snack bowls, she'd placed out this morning. It was utter pandemonium and Allie loved it. She dug out a vase, added water, and placed the colorful autumn bouquet on the center of the kitchen island.

"Please help yourselves to drinks! I have red or white wine and beer and sodas in the fridge. Make yourselves at home. I'll need a volunteer for kitchen help. Any takers?" she asked.

Casey quickly stepped in to claim her spot in the kitchen. "Me," she said, waving her hand. Casey was dying to corner Allie and pry information out of her. They got busy, gathering what they needed to complete the food prep.

"You didn't adequately describe the sexual magnetism of that hunk of burning love," she admonished her friend as she dramatically fanned herself. "What the heck Allie, he's perfect. You've been holding back on me, and now it's time to spill the beans," she hissed at her friend, glancing to make sure she wasn't overheard.

"You didn't ask," Allie said, tongue in cheek.

"Let's not get technical here. As your best friend I shouldn't have to pry that kind of information from you. OMG, Allie, I hope I don't start drooling at the dinner table." They looked over to where Zane was sitting with Darcy. She had grabbed his arm and smiled at something he said, causing Allie to feel a jolt of jealousy, a new experience for her and most definitely an unwelcome one. Darcy was the life of the party, something Allie felt she had never been. Maybe that was more to Zane's liking.

"Does he know?" Casey asked.

"Know what?" Allie responded.

"That you're in love with him?"

Allie dropped the spoon she held, and it clattered noisily to the floor. "Don't be ridiculous, Case. I am *not* in love with him," She huffed. *Was she?* She would admit to a crush, but love?

"I'm not buying it. It's me, Casey. Remember me? Your friend since grade school? The one who has been with you through all your crushes and heartbreaks? The one who has your back?" she said practically. "You can't hide it from me, dear one. I'll drop the subject for now, but we *will* revisit the subject at a later date. Your secret is safe with me." She patted Allie on the back in sympathy. They continued in companionable silence, as Allied pondered over what Casey had just said.

Allie's mom chose that moment to join them in the kitchen. Sarah whispered, "Funny, handsome as all get out, and smart as the dickens. I approve."

"Mom, he is my *boss*, not my boyfriend. Behave yourself." Allie grumbled, "What am I going to do with you two matchmakers?"

"I saw the way you two looked at each other. My dear, I have been around the block a few times and I know magnetism when I see it."

"Speaking of magnetism, there seems to be a lot of it going around these days," she deflected. Her mom practically twinkled. "Well, at least I'm not in denial," she swatted her daughter on her behind. "By the way, Casey, doesn't Allie look stunning today?"

"Yeah, how is it that she can make sexy look classy, or maybe it's classy look sexy? I don't know," she laughed.

Pleased, Allie graciously thanked them. Glancing over at the table again, she happened to catch Zane's eye and he smiled and winked at her.

She returned the smile and called out to the group, "Okay everyone, it's almost time to eat. Could I get one of you strong, sexy men to take the bird out of the oven?"

They could barely move after they had finished with the meal. Allie insisted they wait awhile to do the dishes after clearing the table. "We're too full. Let's sit in the living room around the fire and relax a bit first."

A few dozed off on the couch as the rest of the group decided to play charades to work off the meal. Darcy acted out a movie. She flapped her arms like wings, while exuberantly running around the room, then squatted down, trying to act like she was laying an egg for the "nest." Everyone howled. She displayed no self-consciousness, totally relaxed and comfortable in her own skin. You couldn't help but love her.

Allie glanced over at Zane to see if he was falling under Darcy's spell and found that instead of looking at Darcy, he was staring back at her with such desire that it took her breath away. She immediately felt a matching response in her core. Looking away quickly, she finally figured out what Darcy was trying to get them to guess and yelled out *One Flew Over the Cuckoo's Nest*, only to realize too late that the prize for winning was that it would be her turn. *Damn.*

After a dozen rounds it was getting late. Sarah and Pete had left mid-way through the game, the Johnstons soon followed, and Mark and his family left after waking the twins, who had curled up with the dog and fallen asleep on the floor next to the fire.

As Casey helped Clare with her coat, Dugan started growling at the French doors, which quickly escalated into a defensive frenzy. He lunged at the door on his hind legs, scratching at the windowpanes.

"Dugan, down!" Charlie said sternly. Dugan completely ignored him and continued his eerily deep and menacing growl.

Darcy, always on the alert, went to the back door, hand at her holster, to peer outside. She flipped on the back-deck light to illuminate the area. She thought she detected movement at the back edge of Allie's property but couldn't be sure.

"Zane, Charlie, Sam, come with me. You three stay put, and Allie lock the door behind us. Let's check around outside to make sure nothing is amiss. Zane, do you have your gun with you?" she inquired.

"Yes," he replied. He ran to retrieve it from his leather jacket and was the first one out the door. He hadn't gone very far when he spotted the gruesome message. Hanging from the bird feeder was a dead possum with a noose around its neck.

"Darcy," he called out. "Come over here."

"The sick fuck!" Darcy said disgustedly. By this time familiar with the case, she said, "My best guess is that they're trying to intimidate you. If they can get to Allie and you, it might be enough to scare Havers from testifying against Silva. Let's walk the perimeter of the property and see if we can find any evidence."

"I don't like this one bit," Zane said.

"Me either. It's a little too close for comfort. However, I still think it was for show. They're just trying to scare us off," Darcy said reassuringly. "I don't think Allie should be alone tonight. Can you stay here or take her to your place? I'm sure Casey's would be an option as well."

"No, I'll stay here tonight and insist she come to my place tomorrow. She shouldn't be alone, for her emotional sake as well as for her safety. I've got a secure setup. State-of-the-art security system," he said.

After searching the perimeter, Sam returned with a baggie containing a bloody knife. If they were lucky, it would provide them with a good set of prints.

"Got it. Let's go inside," Darcy said.

"I'll break the news to Allie. We'll need to check on Will and his family and warn them as well." Zane said.

CHAPTER 13

"What if that was Harry?" Allie moaned, a few minutes later, referring to her "pet" possum, who came to her birdfeeder and dined on apples every night.

"We can't be a hundred percent sure until Harry returns to your feeder, but it looked pretty mangled to be a fresh clean kill," Darcy said.

"What was the knife for then?" she questioned.

"He more than likely used that to cut the twine when he tied it up and blood got transferred onto the knife."

"I doubt they took the time to hunt and kill a possum. If they wanted to hurt you, they could have very easily; it's obviously for show," Darcy continued to reassure Allie, who had turned white as a sheet.

"But why me? What good will that do them? I'm not testifying against them," she whispered, voice still shaking.

"It's an intimidation tactic to scare anyone involved

with this case. They're trying to get to Will through any means available to them," Darcy said calmly.

Zane made phone calls. The police were on their way, and he attempted to reach Will, but it went straight to voicemail. Concerned, he put in another call to the police to have them stop by Will's house and do a wellness check.

Giving up on trying to reach Will, Zane returned to Allie and crouched down in front of her, taking her hands in his. "Allie, look at me. I want you to listen to me okay? You're safe. The police are on their way. We are armed. I won't leave you alone. Either I spend the night here, or you are coming back with me to my house. Your choice. Darcy is right. If they wanted to hurt you, they could have easily done it. This was an attempt to scare you and, unfortunately, it worked." His voice was soft and calm and low, conveying confidence and encouragement. "I told you before, I will not let anything happen to you."

Two hours later, the police left after taking their statements and looking around the perimeter of her property for any additional evidence they might have missed. They promised to patrol her road during the night. Allie was exhausted, and her nerves were fried. Zane had closed all the blinds and pulled the curtains across the French doors for privacy.

"Where do you want to sleep, Allie? Upstairs in your bed or here on the couch?" he asked.

"Zane, I can't sleep alone tonight. Can you hold me?"

she asked in a small scared voice. His heart ached for her and his blood boiled with anger at the same time.

He pulled her into an embrace. "Don't worry, I'm not letting you out of my sight. Now, let's go upstairs and get some sleep." Giving her one last hug, he took ahold of her hand to lead her upstairs.

Like a zombie, she let him guide her up to the bedroom. "Sit here, Allie." Steering her to the edge of the bed, he had her sit. He squatted down and unzipped her boots, then pulled them off one at a time. He then unbuttoned her silk blouse; the small pearl buttons a challenge for his larger hands. He slipped off the silky garment, revealing her pale peach bra, which barely covered her full, rounded breasts. Her creamy skin was soft under his hands. He helped her stand so he could remove her skirt. It had a back zipper that followed the contours of her buttocks. He was rock hard but steeled himself to stay neutral as he pulled the zipper down over the swell of her rounded backside. *Her back is lovely.* Long torso with slightly curving hips leading to toned and rounded buttocks, covered by a skimpy pair of pale peach panties. He noticed her bare legs were long and shapely, as she stepped out of her skirt, using his shoulders to steady herself.

When she was stripped down to her bra and panties, he pulled back the covers for her and she collapsed beneath them. He pulled his own T-shirt off, followed by his jeans, leaving his boxer shorts on, he climbed into bed beside her. Spooning from behind, he wrapped his arms around Allie and pulled her in close. Breathing in her feminine scent, he felt a primal need to keep her safe. He smoothed her hair back from her forehead as he made soothing noises. "Go to sleep now, I'm here. I'm not going anywhere. You're safe." He kissed the back of her head, nuzzling her softly. Her gentle, steady breathing told him she was already fast asleep.

The following morning, Allie awoke to Zane's steady breath gently stirring her hair. She snuggled into his warm body enveloping her from behind, which felt like a safe cocoon. Still half-asleep, she turned to face him, observing as he slept on undisturbed. She noticed his long, dark lashes fanning his sculpted cheeks, the tousled dark hair on his head, the soft down-like hair on his muscular chest, leading down like an apex over toned abs to the edge of his boxer shorts. She couldn't resist placing her palms against his chest, feeling the hard muscle and soft hair beneath her fingertips. She reached up to trace his cheek with her thumb.

As she gently brushed his hair back from his brow, he slowly opened his eyes to find Allie's intense gaze upon him. Her thick blonde hair was a wild frame around her delicate beauty. Her mane reached well below her breasts and was a tangled riot of loose curls. Her brown eyes were soft and luminous.

"Hi," he said sleepily.

"Hi," Allie said shyly. The terror of the night before was still tucked away beneath the surface of her consciousness.

Allie leaned in and touched her full lips to his. He groaned, and she immediately felt his erection hard against her pubic bone. She pulled back and traced her finger over his lips, causing him to inhale sharply.

"Allie are you sure this is what you want?" he asked. "I'm not sure I can hold back this time."

"Yes, Zane. I want you," she said with equal solemnity.

He pulled her head toward him as he hungrily placed his lips against hers. He reveled in the taste of her as he explored. He coaxed her parted lips further open as his soft tongue thrust deeper. He plunged in and out with a slow, erotic pulse, sending Allie to the brink of delirium.

He unclasped her dainty bra, gently removing it, exposing Allie's soft pink rosebud nipples and full, rounded breasts. He bowed his head to her and took her nipple into his mouth. He began suckling in an ancient rhythm as he cupped her other breast, gently squeezing and tugging on her areola while continuing his suckling. He expertly used his tongue to send shivers of sensation from her breast to her core. He pulled and tugged with his lips, tongue drawing her in and out.

"Please, don't stop," Allie panted. Just when Allie thought she couldn't take another second of this exquisite torture, he moved his hand between her legs.

In a husky voice he said, "You're so wet, I want you to come for me." Quickly parting her labia he started rubbing gently, then began stroking her faster and faster before finally inserting his finger into her vagina. Thrusting in and out, he went deeper and faster, until she exploded in climax. She rode wave after wave of sensation as she writhed against his fingers.

"Oh my God," she cried out.

She pulled Zane's low-slung boxers further down to expose his hard shaft nestled in dark, curling hair. She grasped it in her hand and gently fondled him. With her other hand, she reached behind his penis to cup him gently, sifting and rolling his roundness. He groaned in ecstasy. She slid her hand up and down his engorged erection, quickly picking up the tempo, her grip firm yet soft.

"I need to feel you inside of me," Allie pleaded.

"Are you sure, Allie?" Zane said breathlessly.

"Yes. Please."

He rolled her onto her back, his knees parting her thighs wide. Poised over her, muscles taut, he paused for a moment to look deeply into her liquid brown eyes. He guided his erection and thrust deeply into her vagina. At first, he moved slowly, but as their arousal deepened, he plunged faster and faster into her moist, receptive womanhood.

He panted as he rode her harder and harder. Muscles strained, his buttocks contracting with each plunge, biceps and triceps bulging as he held himself over her, raw and defined, his sweat glistening on his brow. She wrapped her legs around him to hold him tighter against her.

He watched her heavy breasts bouncing with each thrust. He reached out to pull and pinch one nipple as she moaned with a desperate need for release. She was so beautiful in her abandon, he wanted to possess her in a way he didn't understand or recognize. It was mating in a primal way, and he felt a lust far beyond his control. He couldn't wait for her any longer and he climaxed just as she did, calling out her name.

They were transported to another place and time as ancient as life, overwhelmed with rapture. As he spasmed inside, he could feel her vagina pulsating against his penis. She throbbed against his manhood as the waves kept coming.

They lay there spent for some time until Zane said, "Now what was your name again?"

"Very funny." Allie lightly punched him, and he quickly retaliated by tickling her. The feel of his naked manhood no longer erect against Allie's skin was sensuous in another way.

They rolled around the bed, wrestling playfully, naked limbs entangled.

Zane, now drowsy with satiation, rolled over, draping her across his body, and they dozed off into a light sleep. A short time later, Zane woke up and kissed Allie awake, suggesting that they get up and take a shower.

Zane adjusted the water temperature, and watched the warm water cascade over her body, dripping down her full swollen lips, onto her breasts, sliding over her nipples, on down her flat belly. Zane poured some scented bath gel into his palms and began to lather her.

"Turn around," he commanded.

Complying, she turned facing away from him as he seductively massaged her shoulders and back, moving lower until he reached between the cleft of her rounded buttocks and massaged, inserting his finger into her vagina from behind. Her knees felt weak as if they could no longer support her. He gently continued lathering her inner thighs, working his way down her body. He turned her to face him and applied more gel to his hands and repeated the ritual. Starting at her chest, he lathered her breasts, thumb circling her nipples as his large hands cupped and massaged, causing Allie to groan out loud. He continued his tactile exploration, caressing her belly and between her legs, just a brief flirtatious tease promising more to come. Working his way down to her feet, he crouched as she held on to him for stability, lifting one foot at a time, kneading the muscles with strong confident hands.

Allie looked down at Zane and said, "It's your turn."

"I thought you'd never ask." He smiled widely, revealing his dazzling white teeth, the dark unshaven stubble giving him a dangerous quality.

"Oh, Zane, you are way too sexy by far," Allie said, as she slathered her hands with suds and started rubbing his body. Beginning with his shoulders, she worked her way down each arm, kneading his strong biceps, then forearms, grasping each of his hands and gently stroking every finger, thoroughly massaging each digit. She studied his body through lowered lids, noting his broad shoulders, the muscularly defined chest, with water rivulets following the path of his dark hair all the way down to his phallus.

Massaging his nipples and moving down his torso, she reached the apex. Zane was already hard and waiting. He lifted her up into his arms and pressed her against the shower wall. She wrapped her legs tightly around him as he entered. Thrusting powerfully into her like a stallion, his steady staccato rhythm building until he was blindly plunging into her receptive entry. They both came again simultaneously.

With their arms wrapped tightly around each other, they held on for several minutes while the waves from their climax subsided. She loved the feel of her cheek resting against his wet shoulder while the water cascaded down their intertwined bodies. She licked some droplets from his neck. Unwrapping her thighs from around Zane, Allie stood on unsteady legs. He leaned down and kissed her softly. He began raining kisses all over her face, making her giggle.

"I love you," Allie blurted.

Zane suddenly became very still. *Love*, that was the last thing he ever wanted to feel again. Did he love her? He certainly had feelings for her. He missed her when they weren't together. He couldn't wait to see her at work.

"Allie," he said haltingly, "I'm flattered and honored that you could have feelings like that for me. I'm not worthy of it," he said awkwardly.

Allie pushed Zane away, embarrassed at her slip. She had been carried away by her passion and blurted out something she had only just discovered herself.

"You don't have to say anymore, Zane. I understand. I won't make this out to be anything more than what it was: two consenting adults having great sex. I enjoyed it, you enjoyed it, enough said." She tried to put on a brave face while inside wanting to curl up in a corner and cry.

Zane put his finger under her chin tilting her head up so he could look into her eyes. "Allie, you and I know it was much more than that. You just took me by surprise. This is still too new for me to know how I feel about everything. I do have deep feelings for you, Allie. I really do. I'm sorry I wasn't able to respond the way you would have liked, but I'm honest if nothing else, and I never want to lie to you." Feeling suddenly lonely, he tried to pull her back into his arms, but she stiffened up, so he released her.

They exited the shower, each of them toweling

themselves off separately. Allie, embarrassed and quiet now, kept her back to Zane as she quickly donned her robe. He vigorously dried off, returning to the bedroom to retrieve his clothes from the night before.

"I'll meet you downstairs after you're dressed, so we can come up with a game plan," he called to her as he went downstairs.

CHAPTER 14

*W*hen Allie joined Zane in the kitchen, it evoked the previous night's scene and the fear that went with it. Back to reality. Zane had already put the coffee on and was opening cabinets, searching for Kit's food as she weaved in and out through his legs.

"This cat is dangerous," Zane joked.

"Don't I know it," Allie said, trying to match his light tone.

"We're going to ride over to the Havers' house to see if they are there, since I wasn't able to reach them last night. I just tried again and same thing, straight to voicemail," he said worriedly.

"We?" Allie asked, eyebrows raised.

"Yes, Allie, 'we.' You're coming with me. I'm not leaving you alone at this point. We can reevaluate after we have more information," he said firmly.

Walking over, he tilted her head back with his index

finger and kissed her pouty lips, then sucked her lower lip into his warm, moist mouth.

"Allie don't argue about this please," he said quietly.

"I don't want to be alone anyway. I just object to your bossiness," she replied.

"I'll make note of that," he grinned devilishly.

"Do that," she said.

Laughing, he grabbed their jackets from the coatrack and threw Allie's at her, which she managed to catch. He double-checked the locks on the French doors and kept the curtains pulled shut. "Onward," he said. Opening the front door, they headed to his Dolomite-brown Mercedes-Benz.

Pulling into Will's drive, the place looked deserted. After knocking for several minutes and calling out loudly, Zane walked to the front window and tried peering in through the crack in the curtains. He couldn't see much, but it appeared to be abandoned. Zane reached for Allie's hand and intertwining their fingers, he held on as they walked around to the back-yard. Allie discovered it first and cried out, pointing at a busted-out window and back door gaping wide open. Zane released her hand and pulled out his phone, dialing 911 as he walked toward the open door.

He drew his gun and peered inside. It had obviously been ransacked. Kicking the door open wider, he put his index finger to his lips and motioned for Allie to back up against the outside wall of the house as he entered, crouching down and doing a crablike walk to make himself a smaller target.

Zane looked around with dismay at the destruction. Everything appeared to have been pulled out of drawers and shelves and tossed around. The refrigerator had its contents emptied onto the tiled kitchen floor. As he moved further into the house, he soon realized that nothing had come out unscathed. The mattresses in the bedrooms had been sliced through, dressers overturned, curtains ripped from their rods, baby crib toppled over. In bright red lipstick on the bathroom mirror, someone had written, "SNITCHES DIE."

Whoever had been there was now gone. The police arrived moments later with sirens off but lights swirling, and they began to take inventory of the mess before them. Since there was no blood and no bodies at this point, they assumed it was a simple breaking and entering with vandalism. Zane explained that he had been unable to reach his client since yesterday. The threat on the mirror coupled with the dead possum at Allie's last evening indicated something more ominous. He suggested that they might want to consider this a crime scene and possible kidnapping.

The officers looked at each other and agreed to put crime scene tape around to protect any evidence and to call in a forensics team to check for fingerprints and blood that might not be visible to the naked eye. Satisfied with their plan of action, Zane and Allie left the scene.

Discussing their next moves proved frustrating. Zane felt Allie was being arbitrary and stubborn, while she thought he was being bossy and unreasonable. He wanted her to stay at his house until things calmed down, and she thought they would be just as secure at her house. Zane argued that he had a state-of-the-art security system, with cameras covering his whole property. Every door, window, or point of entry was monitored 24/7. In addition, he could observe everything from inside the house to see who came and went, and he could even surveil from a distant location. He argued that it was impossible for her old farmhouse to be as safe as his home since he had designed it with security in mind.

"What about Kit Kat?" she asked contrarily.

"What about her? We put her in her crate, buy a new litter box, and move her right on in," he said reasonably.

"What about my birds and squirrels?" she asked, losing steam.

"Allie, they will find another source of food supply. They'll understand after I leave them a note explaining," he said, trying to get her to smile.

She did smile slightly. "I'll have to pack some clothes and shoes."

"Of course. We can go back to the house now and pick up Kit, and you can grab a few things. The sooner we get you out of there, the better. Deal?" he asked, proffering his hand.

"Deal," voice a little wobbly, she shook on it.

～

*A*llie cried softly as she closed the front door of her farmhouse, not knowing when she would return. Kit made her displeasure known, howling from her crate in the backseat of Zane's SUV.

Zane was all business now, determined to get Allie to his house as quickly as possible. "All set?" he asked. Suddenly he noticed her tears. "Hey, you." Turning her head and wiping her tears with his thumb, he coaxed her to look at him. "You'll be back. It's not forever, it's just for now. It won't be so bad. I promise I won't hog the TV remote," satisfied when he got a small smile for his effort. "When we get to the house you should start making phone calls to your family and friends, filling them in on what's going on," he suggested.

She nodded, then took a deep breath, as if shaking off the gloom, and turned around to the howling Kit and said, "Kit Kat, it's just a little change of scenery here. No worries." Then they pulled onto the road, headed to their new temporary home.

CHAPTER 15

"Is this what you were referring to when you said, 'bachelor pad'?" Allie asked incredulously. The wrought-iron security gate nestled between two stone pillars swung inward, allowing them to drive through. It could be better described as a modern-day manor. She had thought the lake house was impressive, but it was nothing compared to this large contemporary home.

As they approached the house, the cobblestone drive merged into a courtyard with a sculptural metal fountain in the center. The house sat on a wooded lot with mature trees surrounding it. The entire façade was one of straight lines—glass, metal, and stone. The front entrance was in the rectangular center structure, which was two stories high. The design of glass and stone allowed one to view the open staircase that led from the foyer to the upper level.

The four-car garage branched off to the right. As

they pulled into the garage Allie exclaimed, "Oh my God, if you looked in a dictionary under 'man cave' there would be a photo of your garage."

"Ya think?" Zane asked playfully.

In addition to his convertible Spider, he had a motorcycle, an ATV four-wheeler, two kayaks, a snowmobile, and two bicycles. They began to unload, Kit Kat still complaining in her crate. As the garage door closed, Zane entered the combination on the keypad to his back door and opened it. Next, he entered the code into his alarm system to disengage it.

Allie lugged the cat carrier in and said encouragingly, "Here we are Kat. We're on a mini vacation. You're going to love it here." Kit yowled her displeasure. Zane brought in the litter and box so they could set things up for Kit right away. The sooner they let her out of the crate, the better.

Stepping inside from the garage entry, Allie caught her breath. Setting the crate down, she looked up at the two-story open foyer and dazzling chandelier. Marble floors in the entryway segued with wood throughout the rest of the downstairs. Directly in front of her was a pewter metal staircase that had a landing halfway up, before sharply turning at a right angle to continue the rest of the way to the open loft area. Observed from the inside, she could see the glass front wall and the supporting wall to the left, which was stone all the way from the downstairs floor to the high ceilings in the upper level. To the right of the entryway doors was a lighted rectangular fountain with water cascading down from the stone wall into the well below. The open floor plan allowed her to peer into the living room.

A large modern sectional sofa in a neutral color with bright pillows faced a television built into a granite wall. Bright patterned rugs over hardwood floors added splashes of flair. The open design made the foyer and living room one continuous space, with the living area flowing into the dining room into kitchen in a large L shape. A see-through, two-sided fireplace sat between the living and dining areas.

"This is spectacular, Zane," she enthused. "I've never seen anything quite like this."

"I'm glad you like it, Allie. That's important to me. I actually helped design it," he said modestly.

"Seriously?" she said, eyes widening. "You never cease to amaze me."

"Let's go ahead and put her litter box in the laundry room," he said, turning right and heading toward the back of the house, flipping on lights as he went. Sliding open a gray barn door, he revealed the dream laundry room. It was equipped with loads of shelving and racks, iron and ironing board, baskets and bins, a sink, and a front-loading washer and dryer.

Placing the cat crate down, Allie poured litter into the box and then lifted the latch to let Kit Kat out to explore. Tentatively, she stepped out and immediately sniffed at the box. Zane got down on his haunches to offer reassurance. "Hey, Miss Kitty, let's take a look around. What do you say?" Scratching her in her favorite spot behind the ears, curiosity got the better of her and she waltzed out the door to check out her surroundings.

Zane continued giving Allie a tour of the house, with Kit trailing along. Allie loved the flow of it all. The downstairs master bedroom with a fireplace and large *en suite* was highlighted by a four-person jacuzzi and walk-in shower made of marble tiles with an all-glass front. There was a long bench, which ran the length of the shower, and a shower head at each end. The his-and-hers sinks were made of marble, and the long white vanity beneath had loads of custom storage space. The walk-in closet was as big as a small bedroom. The décor of grays and cream, along with the artwork providing dramatic splashes of color, had a soothing effect.

The back wall of the bedroom featured four French doors leading out to the pool and patio area and hot tub. The inground pool and patio also boasted the requisite pool house and was beautifully landscaped. A cedar arbor full of the now-dormant twisted vines of wisteria covered a portion of the courtyard.

After finishing the downstairs inspection, Zane carried her suitcase up the staircase to the second level. The loft was presently being used as his office, study, and library, with one entire wall floor-to-ceiling book-shelves. Through the doors of the front glass façade was a wrap-around balcony, which looked like the perfect place to sit and relax with a good book. Skylights in the ceiling provided a sense of being in a treehouse, which delighted Allie. She could totally visualize this as a writer's paradise.

Allie leaned over the open railing, looking down into the foyer. "Unbelievable."

There was an open doorway at the back of the room leading into the guest quarters. Zane led her there to drop off her bags. "Allie this is your room. I would love for you to join me in my bedroom, but I don't want to make any assumptions and you still need a place to call your own. The upstairs will be your personal apartment. I will only enter if invited," he said earnestly.

Allie reached out and touched his arm, "Zane, it's all so much right now. I feel like my life has been taken over by the winds of fate and I've completely lost my bearings." It was all she could come up with.

Allie explored her new space and could not resist diving onto the inviting bed. She rolled onto her back and looked at her surroundings. Not in a million years could she have pictured herself in this lap of luxury. Too bad it was under these circumstances.

Her bedroom featured a gray stone fireplace with neutral walls. A balcony off the bedroom allowed a view of the pool below. The king-sized bed was topped with restful soft grays and darker gray pillows. The large bright floral oil paintings added drama to the cool tones. She, too, had an *en suite* with a smaller Jacuzzi and walk-in shower. It was luxurious by any standards, with all glass doors, granite from floor to ceiling, a bench, and an extra-large shower head. The sink was modern and sleek, with pewter fixtures and the wall behind it all mirrors. She most definitely would not be roughing it in the physical realm.

Allie glanced at Zane and saw he was studying her intently. She patted the bed beside her, inviting him to join. He wasted no time in diving in beside her. Rolling onto his side, he propped his head on his hand, just looking at Allie with a warmth that comforted and aroused at the same time. She turned on her side to face him.

"Hi," he said, reaching out to brush his thumb across her lips.

"Hi," she returned, nipping his thumb gently with her teeth before drawing it into her mouth and sucking on it. His eyes darkened with desire as she continued teasing him with her tongue.

"Is there anything I can do to make things easier for you, Al?" he asked.

"You are going above and beyond the call of duty," Allie replied softly, after releasing his thumb.

"It doesn't feel like enough. If it weren't for this case, you would be living your normal life, with family, horses, cat…. I feel responsible for taking that from you," he said solemnly.

"In no way, shape, or form do I blame you. You are no more responsible than my shoe," she said adamantly. "Don't you dare take this on. You are just as much a victim of this mess as I am, and I won't hear it said any other way. You got that?" she said.

"I love it when you're mad. Your eyes get all sparkly and bright," Zane said.

"You're not going to deflect here, Mr. Dunn. No matter what happens, you need to know that you didn't cause this. There is nothing you could have done any differently."

"Whatever," he said. She knew he was not convinced.

"Zane," she said threateningly.

"Allie," he returned innocently. He leaned in to kiss her lightly on the lips. There was an immediate response in her core. She deepened the kiss.

"Allie, what am I going to do about you, huh? I need

to keep my wits about me, and you make that near to impossible," he said quietly.

He reached under her sweater to massage her breast, lightly teasing her nipple through her shear silky bra. With her fingers entangled in his thick dark hair, she pulled him toward her for a kiss. He plunged his tongue deeply into her mouth. Soon, he was drawn irresistibly down to where his hand had just been. Pulling the bra aside to take her ripened fruit into his mouth, he drank of her. While suckling, he unzipped her jeans, pulling them down just enough to allow him to reach his hand inside her panties to thumb her labia. Feeling how wet she already was added an urgency to please her.

He tugged her jeans all the way off and tossed them aside. Licking and kissing his way down her flat belly, he arrived at her mound of dark curling hair and dipped his finger just below into her moist center. Parting the lips of her labia, keeping his thumb on her clitoris, he inserted his middle finger into her vagina and stimulated her in multiple ways until she was writhing under his expert hands. He skillfully teased her until she exploded, her body bucking as she spasmed and called out his name.

After her tremors subsided, she reached for his belt and unbuckled it, then slowly unzipped his jeans. She kissed his belly, her lips following the trail of dark hair to his pubic bone until arriving at his large, engorged erection. She used both hands, one to cup his testicles and the other to grasp his phallus. Starting gently, then more forcefully, she pumped until he was thrusting with each pull on his manhood. Her long hair tickled his belly and thighs, creating jolts of sensation. When she licked the tip of his manhood, he erupted in ecstasy and complete abandon.

Allie crawled back up to lay her head on the pillow next to Zane, facing him as he rolled onto his side toward her. He felt completely satiated and content, lying there next to this beautiful creature. Her pale, flawless skin and delicate features made him feel like a warrior wanting to protect his woman. He could stay right here forever, but Allie had different ideas.

"OK, let's go into that fabulous kitchen of yours so you can feed me. How's that sound?" she asked.

"Not as exciting as laying here with you, but nevertheless a great idea." He smiled and planted one last kiss on the tip of her nose and jumped out of bed. "How does my signature grilled cheese sandwich and canned tomato soup sound?"

"Like a gourmet meal at the moment," she laughed.

"Great. I'll meet you down in the kitchen."

~

*A*llie entered the kitchen just as Zane was ladling the soup into two ceramic bowls. Already on the counter were two buttery grilled sandwiches with cheese oozing out from between the thick browned bread.

"Looks yummy." Allie said, sitting at the bar.

"My specialty. I feed this to all of my lady friends. Hooks them every time." He winked at her.

"Well, I'll make sure to resist," Allie retorted.

"Don't blame you for trying." Coming up behind her with the soup, he set the bowls down and sprinkled

Parmesan cheese and croutons on top. Wrapping his arms around her waist, he hugged her tight to his chest, sticking his nose in her hair and inhaling deeply. "I would like to bottle your scent so I could bring it out to smell on those lonely nights when you're not in my arms."

"Food, Zane, food. Stay focused." She picked up her soup spoon and dug in. "I never thought soup from a can could taste so good."

"See, I told you women can't resist. It's all over for you now, Allie."

"I'm much stronger than that," she quipped back. After lunch, Allie retired to her upstairs bedroom to make a few calls. Kit jumped on the bed and began kneading the comforter. Allie sat on an overstuffed club chair. The side table next to her chair had a crystal reading lamp, which she switched on, to offset the gloom. It cast a warm glow over the room.

Now that she was alone, she had time to process all that had happened in the last twenty-four hours. She looked out over the view from her cozy bedroom and shivered. Yesterday she had felt relatively safe in her world, and now she felt uneasy, exposed, and vulnerable. She got up and closed the blinds to the sliding glass doors and checked the lock. Even with all the security, she just couldn't shake the feeling that she was being watched. She had to remind herself that she was not alone. Zane was right downstairs.

She called her mom first. Of course, Sarah had already heard from Casey about the events from the night before. Allie insisted that she was absolutely safe, and that Sarah shouldn't worry.

"Allie, how do you expect me not to worry? I'm your mother," Sarah said, just like Allie was ten years old. She felt like a child again. However, she didn't want to frighten her mom more, so she put on a brave front.

"Mom, the police are involved. We have Darcy investigating, and Zane happens to have a very impressive security system," she offered.

"Honey, I will feel so much better when this trial is over. You should think about finding another career—something safe and boring." Her mother sounded distraught.

"Mom, that is a little extreme, wouldn't you say?" She tried to reason, "This is not the norm for a paralegal."

"I'm just rattled. You're still my baby and always will be. I can't help myself. Please be careful and call me to check in every day."

"Yes, I promise. I love you, Mom." Allie choked up slightly. She wished she were a child again, being held in her mother's arms, safe and innocent of the dangers of the world.

"I love you too, Sweetie," Sarah said.

They ended the conversation, and Allie called Casey and then the Johnstons to let them know what was going on and to make sure the barn was covered in her absence. Laura implored Allie to take care of herself and not give the barn a thought. They had it covered and soon enough she would be back in the saddle again.

"I promise to give Mel extra treats, and I'll give him a hug from you," Laura vowed.

Still feeling weepy, Allie thanked her friend and agreed to keep in touch. After hanging up the phone, she got up from her chair and lay face down on the bed. She buried her head in her pillow to muffle her sobs, then let the dam break loose and cried her eyes out.

She fell asleep that way, and when she awoke it was dark outside. She was disoriented for several seconds before it registered where she was. Glancing at her watch, she saw that it was past seven thirty. Kit Kat was nowhere to be found. Allie got up rinsed her face then went to find her cat and Zane.

She followed her nose to the kitchen, where Zane was busy chopping and dicing, with soft music coming from his sound system. He had a fire going in the fireplace. The table was set for two, with tapered candles lit, a tablecloth, and a plate loaded with various cheeses, prosciutto, salami, and olives. Kit was at Zane's feet, staring up at him adoringly.

"Traitor," Allie said to Kit, who just blinked at her.

"I assume you had a nice nap?" Zane inquired.

"Yes," Allie said, subdued.

Zane could see, from her puffy eyes and troubled expression, that she had been crying.

"Babe, I talked to Darcy while you were napping. She thinks she has a lead on who was behind the break-in at Will's and the dead possum at your place. It's a guy named Bret Duvall. Duvall has been working with Christian Silva for the last several years, on Will's payroll no less. Duvall is involved in drug trafficking, but Narcotics Enforcement hasn't been able to catch him. He and Christian Silva go way back. They have been in frequent contact while Christian has been incarcerated," he explained.

"Darcy also did her own canvasing of the Havers'

neighborhood, and one neighbor saw the family leave for a short time. When they returned, instead of getting out of their car, they immediately backed out and quickly sped away. That was early in the morning on Thanksgiving." He explained further, "Now she's attempting to track down their whereabouts."

"I've tried to reach Will and left several more messages imploring him to call, so I'm hoping to hear from him. He can't skip bail. We can put him and his family in protective custody until this trial is over," he said in exasperation. "Hell, he and his family can stay here for that matter, if I can just convince him to return."

"I just hope Darcy can find them first," Allie said quietly.

"You and me both. The sooner the better. Right now, I would be happy with just a return phone call."

CHAPTER 16

*M*onday morning, they rode into work together. Zane went directly to his office and closed the door. Allie had much to catch up on because of the long holiday. Several hours later, Darcy strode in and asked Stella if she could see Zane immediately. She glanced over at Allie and nodded her head in greeting. When Darcy entered a room, the whole atmosphere became charged. She was not only beautiful, but she exuded the intensity of a coiled snake ready and waiting to strike. She was, quite frankly, like Zane, a force of nature.

A few minutes later, Zane requested that Allie join them.

"Pull up a seat, Al," Zane said. "Darcy has some information to share."

"Well, I was able to track down their general location from their mobile phone records. The last place the Havers cellphone pinged off was a tower about five hours south of here in Ohio. I'm getting ready to head to that location now. The trouble is if I can find them then so can the bad guys." Darcy paced as she spoke.

"That is a terrifying thought," Allie said.

"You got that right," Darcy replied. "I was thinking that after I locate them, the two of you might have a better shot at convincing them to come in for their safety."

"Call us when you get there and keep us apprised of the situation." Zane offered, "I am willing to do whatever it takes. If you need me there, I can be there. I just need to make arrangements for Allie."

"Whoa," Allie protested. "What do you mean 'arrangements'? If you go, I'm going with you. We're in this together. I'd be a wreck sitting here while you're out there putting yourself at risk."

"There's no way, Allie," Zane replied.

"Yes, Zane, there is a way. It's simple, I get in the car, you get in the car, we drive together." She spoke as if explaining something to a child.

"Allie, I can't take that risk," he said, his voice calm and reasonable.

Darcy interrupted them. "I will let you two figure that out. Zane, I will definitely take you up on your offer to join me, and you as well, Allie, if you two decide it's for the best. I need to round up my posse and hit the road."

"I have a few things to do here at the office that will tie me up for today," Zane said, "but I'll drive down as soon as you locate them unless something happens. In which case, I'll just have to jump in the car and come immediately."

"Great, I'll be in touch." And with that she left.

"Zane, I *am* going," Allie said threateningly.

"Allie, I am not going to sit here and argue with you. No, absolutely not. You're wasting your breath trying to convince me. Subject closed."

"Darcy is an ex-cop. I'm sure she knows how to keep us safe," she said, equally stubborn.

"No!" Zane repeated.

Allie rose and angrily stormed out of his office.

The ride home was a silent one, both fuming. They drove through the gates and entered the house without uttering one word. Allie went directly upstairs to her room, intending to skip dinner altogether and not come out for the rest of the night. Zane retired to his room to make some calls in private.

∾

The next day, the silence continued as they drove together to the office with little conversation. They were courteous but cool with one another. Neither had any intention of budging from their stances.

Allie kept in touch with her mom and Casey but missed seeing them in person. She felt trapped. If this went on much longer, she was going to insist on getting her car and reclaiming her independence. To hell with it. She felt that if they were going to do something to her, they would have already. Darcy hadn't had any luck in locating the Havers yet, but she thought she was closing in.

It was Friday and with a minimal amount of conversation, they had decided to pick up a pizza on the way home. Allie called it in, and they went through the pick-up window to retrieve it. Allie decided to broach the subject of her car.

"Zane, this has been very generous of you and all, but I think it's time that I pick up my own car. If they were going to attempt to get to me, they would have tried by now. I'm getting claustrophobic. We're at each other's throats. I'm going stir-crazy. I want to see my mom. I want to see Mel."

"Are you serious?" Zane said.

"One hundred percent," she retorted. "I'm a free woman, the last time I checked. You can't hold me hostage."

"You're being ridiculous. Nothing has changed. Do you think they just decided to forget the whole thing? They left a gruesome calling card dangling from your bird feeder. Have you forgotten?"

"No, I haven't forgotten. I'm not suggesting that I go back to the farmhouse to live. I'm just saying that I think I could have use of my own car. I feel like I'll lose my mind if I don't get some of my life back. You said it yourself," she reasoned. "They were only trying to scare me and send a message to Will."

"At the time, I was trying to put you at ease. You were terrified, Allie, and rightfully so. Do you think I am enjoying this house arrest? I'm here to tell you that I'm not," he said.

"At least you're in your own home with your own things around you and your own car," she said with irritation.

"I understand all that, but you have to be reasonable," he said with barely veiled impatience.

"Reasonable?" she exclaimed. "I'll tell you what's reasonable. Reasonable is that I get to have a say in my own destiny. Reasonable is that I am not a child, and when I say I want to go with you to meet with Will, that I'm the one to make that decision. Reasonable is that, after all this time with no more threats, I get to drive myself to work and back." Her anger was building. "How dare you tell me to be reasonable."

"Allie, there is no decision to be made here—the answer is no!" he said imperiously.

"We'll see about that, Mr. Dunn," she said fuming.

He shook his head in exasperation but held his tongue. There would be no reconciliation tonight.

~

Zane was in a deep sleep when his cellphone rang. The call coming in was from Will; he was immediately on high alert. "Will, where the hell are you?" he barked.

"They have Camilla!" Will said. "Zane they have Camilla!"

"Try to calm down, Will. Tell me what happened," Zane said.

"We've been in hiding and going out late at night when we need supplies. Camilla went out about an hour ago to get some food for the kids and she hasn't returned," Will said with alarm.

"Damn, not good news. Will, I'm assuming you've tried her cellphone?"

"Yes, repeatedly."

"You must let us do our job to protect you. Where are you? You have to come in. We can't protect you out there, you must see that. You're putting your family at greater risk by hiding from those who can help you. You, Camilla, and the kids can stay here once she returns, or at a safe house, but you must return," Zane said.

"I don't trust the cops. With the exception of you and Allie, I don't trust anyone. Christ, Zane, Camilla's own brother is behind all of this," Will said in anguish.

"You have to trust someone. You can't do this alone. Think about your family. How can you protect them out there? How do you think they found you?" Zane asked.

"I have no idea," Will said dejectedly. He continued, "We went out early Thanksgiving for something we forgot and thank God, we decided to go as a family. When we returned home, we surprised the intruders. When we drove up, we could see someone inside, so I gunned it and got the hell out of there. They didn't have time to follow us. I thought it was a clean getaway." He explained, "I need some time to think. I'm crazy with fear for Camilla. I hope that they contact me, and I will make a trade, me for Camilla. I don't care anymore. I just want my family safe," he said. He was desperate and sounded like he was unraveling.

"Don't make any trades, dammit," Zane said. "Will, get ahold of yourself—if you turn yourself over, you're a dead man for sure. How do you know that your family will be safe after that? There are no guarantees. You may not have any faith in the cops, but you definitely can't trust these criminals to keep your loved ones safe. Let's hope that Christian has enough conscience left that he wouldn't allow harm to come to his own sister."

Zane heard a child's voice in the background. "Daddy, where is Mommy?"

"She went out to get you a treat. Go back to sleep, little guy," Will said, voice breaking.

With his gut wrenching, Zane said quietly, "Please come to your senses. I understand it feels like a risk either way, but you must weigh the odds. Which is the bigger risk, Will? Think about it."

"I've got to go. I'll call back later." He abruptly ended the conversation.

Zane got up and threw some clothes on. Sleep was an impossibility now.

~

Rummaging around in the fridge, Zane took a piece of leftover pizza and stuck it in the microwave. He grabbed a beer and twisted the cap off. Taking a large swallow, he downed a third of the bottle in one swig.

Zane felt weary all the way to his bones. A simple twist of fate and your whole life can change in an instant. It was an utter waste of time to play the "what if" game but hard not to. He felt he was failing Allie right now, unable to give her what she needed. He hated the feeling of being a jailor, and he knew she felt he was unsympathetic, but it was far from the truth. He just didn't see any other way to approach this. He needed to keep her safe and felt that he was the best one to provide that protection. He couldn't bear the thought of something happening to her. She just had to trust him, but he knew her restlessness could cause her to act impulsively. He really couldn't blame her, but he saw no way around it. He couldn't risk her being anywhere near Will and his family.

Just before sunrise, Zane received word from Darcy that she'd located Will. They were holed up in a Motel 6 off I-75. He told her about Will's phone call and warned her again to wait for him and to be careful. "I'll be on the road within an hour," he promised.

Sometime during the night, it had begun to snow. There was already an accumulation of an inch or two, with reports calling for another eight inches throughout the day. The sky was spitting out big fat white flakes that were falling softly down. There was no wind to speak of yet, but that was supposed to change as the day wore on. Zane wished he had time to enjoy it. This was his favorite type of snowfall—no ice, no wind, no sleet, and temperatures hovering around thirty degrees. At least he was heading south, so he should be driving out of the weather rather than into it.

After packing an overnight bag, he left a note for Allie and commanded that she stay inside the house and not venture out anywhere. He could only imagine how this was going to go over with Allie, but it was the best he could do.

When Allie woke up, she looked out the French doors and saw the snow coming down in big flakes the size of nickels. So beautiful. After throwing on her robe, she went downstairs to make a pot of coffee. The first thing she spotted was the note from Zane.

"Allie, I received a call from Darcy and had to leave at dawn this morning. DO NOT LEAVE THE HOUSE! I will inform the office you won't be in. Annika will cover for you. I will stay in touch. Love, Zane." Her heart skipped a beat at the word *love*. Love? Was that just a standard sign-off, she wondered, or was it an endearment? Her anger of the past several days seemed petty now, in the face of the danger Zane was walking into. Please let him be safe.

CHAPTER 17

Allie sat pondering the note and her options while drinking her coffee. She knew she would go crazy sitting at the house, just waiting to hear from Zane. With Will and everyone else out of the state, she was sure no one would be concerned with her if they'd even been interested to begin with. Getting up, she fed Kit then started scrounging around in Zane's kitchen drawers, looking for the keys to his Alfa. Just a quick trip out to see her horse and feel normal again. With that plan in mind, Allie jumped into the shower and dressed in a sweater, blue jeans, boots, and heavy parka to go out to the barn. At the last minute she remembered Zane's gun and stuffed it in her tote bag.

Settling into the Alfa she made a quick call to Laura from her cell to let her know she was stopping by the barn. Allie was a little worried about how such a small car would handle in this weather, but she would be extra cautious. She slid a little on the drive but didn't let that deter her. Hanging back so the gates could swing in, she exited the property and the gates swung closed behind her. Freedom! However, the joy was tempered by worry for Zane; the pleasure felt hollow and she really didn't feel very free. She tried to shake off the anxiety for now and focus on her driving. She couldn't wait to see Mel.

The lane to the barn hadn't been plowed yet and there was already about four inches of snow. She fish-tailed slightly, making her way to the barn. She loved how quiet the world seemed during a snowfall and immediately after. There was a hush when everything was blanketed in white. She slid open the barn door and nearly cried when she heard Mel's greeting.

"Oh, Mel, how I've missed you." Wrapping her arms around his neck, she buried her face in his warmth.

"Let me go get you some treats." As she entered the tack room, Daniel and Jack roused from their warm comfy beds to greet her. "Some watch dogs you're becoming. You must be the fair-weathered kind," she said, taking turns petting them. She gave them each a treat from the bin, grabbed a few more oat cookies for later, and returned to Mel's stall.

Pulling up a bucket, she flipped it upside down and used it for a stool as she sat by Mel's head. Leaning back against the stall door, she said, "Mel, you wouldn't believe the craziness that has become my life." He listened intently, nuzzling her for another snack. Oblig-ing, she held out her hand and he gently took it, with soft lips searching her hand much like an elephant uses his trunk to search for peanuts. She listened to the soothing sound of him crunching his treat. He blew out of his nose and lips, an expression of contentment. She didn't know how long she sat like that, mind blank, just present to the smells of the horses and barn, the peacefulness, the sounds of the horses munching on their hay. She became aware that she was cold and stiffening up; it was time to return home.

She gave Mel one last hug. "I can't promise how soon I can get back, but it won't be too long. I love you, Big Guy," Allie wiped a tear from her cheek with her gloved hand as she pulled the barn door shut. She had forgotten to bring a windshield scraper, so she just used her glove to swish off the snow. Fifteen minutes later, she was pulling in the gate to Zane's place. It was so odd coming home alone, without Zane here to greet her, even eerie. She couldn't let her imagination run away with her or she might slip through the rabbit hole. Time to buck up. She patted the tote bag to reassure herself, suddenly very appreciative that she had a gun and sort of knew how to use it.

Pulling into the second stall, the garage door closed behind her and she used the code and entered the house. The large expanse of front windows, so striking and beautiful before, now made her feel like she was a specimen in an aquarium.

She fed Kit and made a peanut butter and jelly sandwich, taking it upstairs to her bedroom to eat. She closed the blinds and decided to snuggle in with a good book. She called Casey and set up a time to meet her the next day to go for breakfast and then on to the farmhouse to retrieve a few more changes of clothing and her car.

Casey said, "Are you sure it's safe, Allie?"

"I went to the barn today with no trouble, and wouldn't it make sense that they would have followed the Havers, which is who they're really after?" she said convincingly.

"Well, if you're sure. I'll be there at Zane's around 8:00 tomorrow morning. I'll text you when I get there."

"Thank you. I don't know what I'd do without you Case. I'll be ready. I can't wait to see you," she said, fighting to keep herself from weeping.

"Me too. See you then," Casey said, and disconnected.

～

*L*ater in the evening her cell phone rang. It was Zane.

"Zane," Allie said eagerly.

"Allie," Zane said tenderly. "What are you doing right now?"

"Sitting in the bedroom, curled up in the chair reading. I lit a fire in the fireplace," she said.

"I'm sitting in a diner with Darcy. We're discussing strategy," he said.

"It was weird coming back to the house alone." Immediately realizing her blunder, she could only hope that he wouldn't pick up on it. No such luck.

"Coming back?" he asked in a deadly flat tone.

"Please don't make a big deal out of this. I figured everyone is out looking for Will, so nobody could possibly be interested in me at this point. I decided to go to the barn for a quick visit. I took your gun...I'm back. Everything went fine. I'm safely tucked in again. Don't be mad."

"The Alfa, I presume?" he asked, dangerously quiet.

"Yes," she answered in a small meek voice.

"I knew I should have taken those damn keys. Allie, how could you? Do you know who and what we are dealing with here?" he asked rhetorically.

"I know Zane, but nothing happened. I'm home now. I miss you," she said quietly, taking the wind from his sails.

"I miss you too, Allie. You have no idea. I just can't have you taking any more chances like that. Okay?"

Allie crossed her fingers and said, "Yes." She had no intention of telling him about her date with Casey tomorrow. There was no need to worry him, they would just do a quick in-and-out of the farmhouse. She had only brought several days' worth of clothing, and she needed some warmer things as well.

"Zane, please be careful. Kit and I need you," she said, her voice like a caress.

"I will, and Allie, I don't need any added distractions of worrying about you. Please don't do anything more to put yourself at risk," he said.

"Call me," she said.

"I will. Be good. By the way, how is my baby?" he asked.

"You mean Kit?"

"No, my Alfa," Zane said.

"Oh, your baby is just fine. Nothing a plunger can't pop out." He laughed for what felt like the first time in a week.

"Goodnight, Al. I wish I were there to tuck you in," he said.

"Me too. Talk to you soon?" she asked.

"Yes. Sleep tight." And he hung up.

Allie felt empty after they disconnected. She had so wanted to tell him she loved him, but she had held back. She would figure that out later. Right now, she would get into the Jacuzzi and try to relax her tense muscles. She threw a few more logs into the bedroom fireplace and then ran the water for her bath. She put on some soothing music and slipped out of her clothes, glancing at her body in the mirror. She looked too thin, her eyes a bit hollow. She pinned her hair up to avoid getting it wet, climbed in and turned on the jets full blast so that the water pulsated against her neck and shoulders. She leaned back and let the moment take her away.

Later in bed, going over her conversation with Zane, she felt a tiny bit guilty for misleading him about tomorrow. But, she rationalized, after she retrieved her clothes from home, she would comply with his wishes. After all, it really was for her safety. Tomorrow they would have breakfast, a quick in-and-out of the farmhouse for clothes, pick up her car, then she would put herself back in her luxurious cage and throw away the key. She reached over and turned off the reading lamp and had a restless night's sleep, interspersed with troubling dreams that were dark and full of danger.

CHAPTER 18

Zane and Darcy, dressed all in black, circled around to the back of the motel after dark. Both carried their weapons close to their sides, on the alert for any unusual movements. Camilla hadn't returned and there had been no word or demands from anyone. They swiftly knocked on the door and called out to Will. He cracked the door with the chain still on to peer out, making sure it was Zane. He quickly unlatched the lock and they entered.

Three pairs of dark brown eyes stared at Zane and Darcy from one of the double beds. The baby had been crying a moment before, but the surprise at seeing these two strangers in the room distracted him enough to stop. The room was complete chaos, but with a family of five basically living in a thirteen-by-twenty-five room, there was not much they could do about it.

"Any contact yet?" Darcy asked, taking charge.

"No," Will replied. "I want to trade myself for Camilla." He repeated his earlier plan. "I should have gone to the store myself. I never should have let her talk me into her going out alone. The kids were fussy, and the baby was asleep, so we didn't want to haul them out. She felt like I could protect them here better than she could, and we really didn't think they knew where we were hiding. She was so insistent that she be the one to go. I really messed up." He buried his face in his hands, crying quietly.

"You'll drive yourself crazy thinking about the 'should haves,'" Darcy said. "I should know—I'm a pro at it. Stay strong, Will. We will hear from them."

"For now, we just wait," Darcy continued. "Zane and I will be outside in my van watching your room. We've been discussing this, and we may need to play along with your idea, trick them into thinking you're giving yourself up in order to get to Camilla. So far, they must not have been able to get Camilla to give up your location. We hope that it stays that way."

She rustled around in her backpack and pulled out a UHF radio transmitter listening device. "I'm going to set this up, in case they try to contact you. The call will be transmitted to our receiver, which is set to this frequency. We'll be able to hear everything. All you have to do if you get a call is to make sure you answer with your speakerphone on and, of course, mute the sound on the TV."

"One of our concerns is that we don't know how many flunkies Duvall has at his disposal. We have two of my men watching the front for any suspicious activity, and we're all set up with two-way radio transceivers. I still wish you would consider bringing in the cops, but at this point I don't want to make that call for you. I'm just glad you let us get involved," she said.

"I'm trying to hold it together for the kids, but I feel like I'm ready to crack." Will's voice was edgy.

Darcy took another look at the three little ones and put her gun down on the small desk. She went over picked up the baby and began cooing and talking baby talk. "Hey, little one." Looking at the oldest, who was four, she asked, "What's your baby brother's name?"

"Nicolas," he said.

Looking at the middle child, a beautiful girl who looked to be around two, she said, "What is your sister's name?"

"Isabella," he replied again.

"And what's your name?" she asked gently.

"Daniel." He smiled at her but seemed suddenly quite bashful.

Darcy sat on the edge of the bed, still holding Nicolas, and wrapped her free arm around the tiny shoulders of Daniel. "You're being such a good big brother. I see that you've been playing with your little sister. What is your favorite thing to play?" she asked.

"Hide and seek. Do you want to play with us?" he asked hopefully.

"I would love to, but I can't right now. I will take you up on it another time. Do you know how to play "I See Something in This Room?" she asked.

He shook his tiny head, with the dark mop of curls bouncing.

"I think we have time for that." Looking at Zane, she raised her eyebrows in question.

"Sure we do, Buddy," he said, sitting on the second bed facing them.

"I'll go first," Darcy said. She looked around the room, trying to find something obvious to a four-year-old and found just the thing. "I see something in this room, and it is pink and white and soft. It has long ears, too."

Daniel scrunched up his brow and looked around the room until he lighted upon the pink bunny sitting on a chair. "The bunny!" he exclaimed, excitedly pointing at the stuffed animal.

"You got it already. Wow, Daniel, are you sure you haven't played this before?" Zane asked.

"No, I promise," he said innocently. "Can I do one now?"

"Sure," Zane said.

"I see something in the room and it's bwack," he said, staring right at Zane's black knit hat. Darcy and Zane pretended to look around the room while Daniel's eyes sparkled with delight.

"Black, huh? I don't know about you, Darcy, but this one has me stumped," Zane said.

"Me too," Darcy said, while exaggerating her perusal of the room.

Just then, the little girl shyly pointed at Zane's hat and said, "At." Daniel clapped his hands in delight.

"Sissy, you got it! You guessed it!" Jumping off the bed, he began to run around the room with glee saying, "She got it! She got it! Sissy guessed."

"She sure did. Your sister must be pretty smart," Zane said.

"Can we do another one?" Daniel asked.

"I'm so sorry Daniel, but we have to go now. Maybe you and your sister can play it without us," Darcy said.

Zane and Darcy both stood up to leave. Darcy bent over to put Nicolas back on the bed in a little nest they had made for him, and she asked Isabella for a hug. Isabella held out her pudgy little arms and wrapped them around Darcy's neck. Darcy felt her eyes tearing up. So innocent. We all start out this way—pure, trusting. Why do people become monsters, she wondered, not for the first time? She straightened and composed herself before turning back to the men.

"We'll be right outside watching your door, Will. If you get any calls, just remember we'll be listening. We will give two light knocks on the door to signal to let us in. We can then write notes and communicate with you, if it comes down to negotiations," Darcy instructed.

"Any questions?" Zane asked.

Obviously agitated, he replied that he understood, and they slipped from the room.

Around three AM, the two men on duty at the front of the hotel, radioed to report that a taxi had entered the parking lot. There was a woman who fit Camilla's description in the front seat, and they were driving around the back lot toward them.

A moment later, they heard Will's cell ring and he answered.

"Hello," Will answered breathlessly.

"Will," she cried.

"Camilla. Thank God you're alive! Where are you? Do they still have you? My darling," he said sobbing.

"Mommy! Mommy!" They heard the children cry out in the background.

"I'm in a taxi. They let me go and I'm here now. I'm going to be knocking on the door in a few seconds. I didn't want you to think it was them," she said in obvious distress.

"Wait right there. Zane is in the parking lot. He'll meet you at the taxi. Wait for him to come and get you," he begged.

"I'll wait," Camilla said.

Zane and Darcy jumped out of the van and ran to the waiting taxi. They hustled Camilla out of the vehicle and into the motel room. They all gathered anxiously to hear Camilla's story and to question her.

"Tell us exactly what happened, Camilla," Darcy said calmly and kindly.

After the emotional greetings from her husband and children, Camilla was sitting in a chair holding Nicolas, with the other two clinging to her legs. Camilla had an ugly gash on her cheek and swelling around her left eye. She looked like she had taken a tumble and seemed to be moving cautiously, as if avoiding pain. Will stood beside her, with his hand protectively squeezing her shoulder.

"After I left the grocery store, I was driving down the road and a car came up close behind me and began following. At first, I thought they were tailing so close because I was driving very slowly due to the weather, but then the car accelerated and bumped me. I lost control and then righted myself, only to have them ram me again. Then I knew it was intentional. My car spun out of control on the ice and I went into the ditch. I locked my doors, but two men approached and pointed their guns at me, so I knew I had to open the car door."

She was wringing her hands and trembling as she recounted her experience.

She continued, obviously distraught. "I fell as they pulled me from my vehicle and dragged me to their car. I stumbled and hit my head against the door as they forced me into the back seat. I began to struggle and one of the men hit me in the face with the butt of his gun and then got in beside me. The other one got in the driver's seat and started driving."

"Were you able to get a good look at them?" Darcy asked.

"No, they both had on ski masks, so I never saw their faces."

"Any distinguishing characteristics? I know this is difficult, but I need you to think really hard, did anything stand out, an accent, a scar or mole or even a tattoo, could help us," Darcy said.

"Neither man spoke for the longest time, until they pulled into a deserted rest area and parked. One thing that stood out is that one of the men had a Spanish accent and the other an American one."

"Can you describe the car they were driving?" Zane asked.

"Not really, dark, big SUV of some kind, I'm sorry I'm not good with this."

"Then what happened?" Darcy asked.

"I began crying, pleading with them not to take me from my babies. They told me they just wanted me to get a message to my husband. The message was to tell him that snitches die. That if he showed his loyalty to my brother, he would not have to see his family die, but if he snitched, he would live to see us tortured and killed first and only then would he be put out of his misery."

"Did they say who the message was from?"

"No. I just assumed..." Camilla began to quietly weep as she continued. "They threw me out of the car and drove away. I had my cellphone, so I managed to call a taxi. I watched to see if anyone followed us, but it was deserted and there were no other car lights anywhere. I had the taxi driver take a few detours to be sure, and there was no one." Now her weeping had turned into sobbing as she rocked herself.

Will said protectively, "She needs to rest and forget about this for the night. Our children need their mother's attention. Please leave us for now."

Zane replied, "Will, you were released on a million dollars bail. You're not allowed to leave the state. Those were the terms of the agreement. Right now, you're breaking the terms of the bail arrangement. We can transport you back to my home now and put you up there until we can find a safe house for you and your family. We have two vehicles that aren't on their radar. I think it's our safest bet for now."

"Can you give us a little time as a family? We need to calm the kids down and Camilla as well. I think we can be ready to go by six," he said, looking at the bedside clock.

Zane and Darcy exchanged glances, and Darcy nodded affirmation to Zane.

"Okay," he confirmed, "we will call you to signal that we are right outside your door with the transportation. You'll get in the van and go with us, and our two men will get your luggage and follow. Only take what you need for the trip back," he instructed.

"Thanks," Camilla said shakily.

"You are safe now, Camilla. We've got you," Darcy reassured her, and they walked back out into the snowy night.

CHAPTER 19

Casey picked up Allie at Zane's front gate at eight o'clock as promised. They settled into their booth at the diner and completely ignored the menus the waitress had left for them. There was so much to catch up on. Allie updated Casey on the latest events happening, which sounded so farfetched that they both ended up hysterical with laughter. Wiping her tears, Casey said, "Why are we laughing?" which caused them to erupt in more merriment.

"Must be a release valve," Allie said.

"Must be. It's just so crazy—it sounds more like a movie than my best friend's life," Casey said. "I've been sick with worry."

"I know. I feel bad for you and Mom. I feel like such a burden. Will my life ever be normal? What is normal anyway? I just feel like my drama-meter is on overdrive this lifetime," Allie said seriously.

"Don't worry about us. Love is a privilege not a

burden. Your mom and I just want you to be safe and happy," Casey said.

"I know Mom wants me to get a 'boring' job," Allie said, using her hands to make quotation marks. They both chuckled over that one.

"So, Allie, how are things on a more personal level with you and Zane?" Casey asked.

"Not to be clichéd, but it's complicated." She sighed. "I have feelings for him.... No.... It's more than that. God help me, Casey, I'm in love with him." Allie covered her face with her hands. "I'm sure he feels something for me, I'm just not sure how much. He said early on that he was not ready to get serious and that he still carries baggage from his first marriage, so I have no clue really." She looked at her friend forlornly and continued. "I must admit at least to you and to myself that I have fallen pretty hard. He's funny, smart, kind, considerate, he's a good listener, compassionate, a great lover. I could go on and on." She laughed at herself.

"Yeah, I'd say you've got it pretty bad," Casey commiserated.

"For now, we just have to get through this mess, hopefully alive," she said.

"Don't even say that," Casey exclaimed. Just then the waitress appeared, and they finally glanced at their menus. Allie ordered a cheese omelet and Casey requested two eggs over easy with wheat toast and a side of bacon. They had already been served coffee and were ready for refills. The waitress came back with a pot of fresh brew and poured, leaving room in the mugs for cream and dropped a handful of the small plastic containers of creamer on the table.

Pensive, Casey studied Allie as she peeled back the foil lid on the creamer and poured it into her cup. She noticed how gaunt her friend looked and the dark smudges under her eyes. Concern clouded her own expression. "You know, Charlie and Sam think you should stay somewhere besides Zane's place. Maybe fly to Florida until everything blows over. You can stay in our condo for free. You know how beautiful it is there. Just think, sitting on the beach, away from all of this crazy shit, right on the gulf. Staying here isn't worth the risk, Allie. I think I agree with them," Casey said.

"I would feel like I was abandoning Zane and Kit Kat," Allie replied.

"You wouldn't be. In fact, it would probably ease Zane's mind to have you far away and safe from danger. If you get hurt or—God forbid—die, you'll really be abandoning him." Quickly reassuring, she said, "Not that we think that'll happen. They want Will, not you. However, if they can use you to leverage the situation, I'm sure they'd have no compunction about doing so," Casey said.

"I'll consider it. I don't want to be naïve about it. I just think my own risks are low here compared to the Havers family," Allie reasoned.

"Well, I'm willing to take some time off to go down with you to help you settle in if you decide to relocate temporarily. I can also help out financially until you get back to work," Casey offered.

"Zane is paying me, of course, for my lost wages. I'm all right for now," Allie said.

"All you would need is transportation and food. We could help you there as well," Casey offered generously.

They decided to drop by the barn before going on to the farmhouse. Casey hadn't visited with Mel for quite some time, and Allie could never get enough of the barn, so she was happy to have two days in a row visiting with Mel. As is the way with lifelong friends, there was a camaraderie that both comforted and buoyed their spirits.

CHAPTER 20

Zane tried calling Allie when they were about an hour from home, annoyed and concerned when she didn't pick up. They'd been driving for several hours and the kids had fortunately fallen asleep almost immediately, with Camilla and Will joining them in dreamland soon after. Darcy was driving her van, with her two men following in Zane's SUV and their other vehicle. She glanced over at Zane when she heard his exasperated sigh.

"Troubles?" she asked.

"I can't reach Allie," he responded, jaw tight.

"She could be in the shower, you know," Darcy said logically. "Give her a few minutes and try again."

"I just don't think she's taking the threat seriously enough. She actually left the house and went to the barn yesterday. I was so pissed off at her," he said. "In my Alfa Romero, no less. In the snow." He had to grin on that one.

"Ha," Darcy exclaimed good humoredly. "Well, it would be hard to be holed up alone like that, and she is probably right that she's not really important to them." She continued, "However, we can't assume anything and it's better to not take unnecessary risks."

"I agree, it's much too serious to take chances or try to second guess what their next move will be," Zane said. "She said my Alfa survived and the damage could be 'plunged out,'" he laughed.

"She is a character, that one." Darcy looked over at Zane to study any reaction to her statement.

"Yes, she is that... among many other things," he answered quietly.

"You know, I hope you don't mind my saying, but the chemistry between the two of you is off the charts. If I've learned one thing, it's that that kind of connection doesn't come along every day, and when it does you have to seize the opportunity for love," Darcy said sounding wistful.

"Sounds like you're speaking from experience," Zane said.

"Truth be told, there's a deeper reason why I left the police force. I fell in love with my partner. It happened pretty unexpectedly and quickly. I think working so closely with someone in often-intense situations day after day accelerates intimacy. Trust develops quickly when you each have the other person's life in your hands. He was charming, handsome, and brave. The best partner anyone could wish for. We got engaged six months after meeting, although we tried to keep our relationship under wraps at work," Darcy explained.

"We picked up a call from dispatch that was for a

domestic situation. We arrived at a volatile scene. The husband had a gun and was threatening to kill his estranged wife and himself. We called for backup and Ryan, my fiancé, began to negotiate," she continued.

"We thought he was about to hand over the gun to Ryan—he had actually been placing it on the ground— when suddenly he pointed it at Ryan and fired a shot. Ryan went down. I leapt at the shooter, and the gun went flying. I was so enraged that I could have killed him with my bare hands. The hardest thing I've ever done was to restrain myself from killing him in cold blood right then and there," she said quietly.

Zane reached over and touched her on the arm and said, "I'm so sorry, Darcy. I can't even imagine what that must have been like."

"I resigned from the force immediately. Nothing mattered anymore. I fought my way back through the guilt, grief and 'what ifs' and came out on the other side. I really don't know how... I like to think Ryan is still with me, pushing me to move on and live my life. I know he never would have wanted me to give up, so I have to honor him by living the life he was robbed of," she said solemnly.

"Darcy," Zane said, "I admire you tremendously. You have come through and still sparkle and are a joy to be around. It means a lot that you shared that story with me."

"Well, I hope you got my message. We never know how much time we have on this earth. Don't squander it. It's better to go for it and fail then to have regret later and wonder what could have been," she said wisely.

Zane gave her a warm smile, "You've given me a lot to think about."

CHAPTER 21

*C*asey and Allie pulled into the lane leading to the farmhouse. It felt surreal, like a distant memory. How could it be that everything had changed so dramatically in such a short time. Jumping out of the car with Casey right behind her, she entered the house. Everything looked the same, but it felt empty. As if there was no life in the home anymore. Allie felt a weird sense of loss. She went upstairs to her bedroom to pack some clothes after directing Casey to empty out the fridge and dump the trash outside in the receptacle. They would put it at the curb before leaving.

Allie packed some warmer clothes and more underwear and a couple pairs of jeans. She threw in some sweaters and wooly socks as well. Grabbing some toiletries and girlie stuff, she headed back downstairs.

As she hit the bottom landing, calling out to Casey and laughing about her heavy load, she saw a stricken look on Casey's face. Her friend yelled at her, "Run!" A masked man had a gun pointed at her friend. She knew he wasn't interested in Casey and she could never run and leave her friend behind. She froze.

"Let her go," Allie said. "I'll do whatever you ask, just let her go."

She dropped her bags and put both hands up, palms facing toward the man in the pose of surrender and said, "I'm the one you really want. Why make this more difficult for yourself, she would just be an unnecessary complication." She knew her cell was in her back pocket, but the gun was in her tote on the passenger seat of Casey's car. *Fuck!*

"I have a better idea." The man in a ski mask shoved some twine toward her. "Here, tie her up," he said.

"Just let her go," Allie pleaded. "She is of no value to you."

He shoved her, snarling, "Shut up and do as you're told." Then, directing his orders to Casey said, "I'm in charge here. You. Sit in this chair." He pointed at the chair and then motioned to Casey with his gun. She complied, white as a sheet, stark terror in her wide eyes.

The man walked over to Casey, studying her intently. "You're a pretty one, hmm?" He stroked her cheek with the barrel of his gun as she trembled.

"Now, don't try to be heroic. Just do as I say, and nobody will get hurt. I'd hate to see anything happen to that pretty face," he said ominously.

"Why bother with us? We are of no value to you," Casey tried reasoning her voice shaky.

"Well, let's see," he said dripping sarcasm. "Lawyer has the snitch, I have the lawyer's beautiful *puta*, what don't you understand?" He laughed.

Looking at Allie, he said, "I knew it was only a matter of time before you would show up here. Not a very smart move on your part, my beauty."

"Please don't do this," Allie begged.

"I said stop talking!" he screamed at her his face reddening.

Allie bent down to tie Casey's hands behind her back as she had been instructed to do, while he watched closely. She only hoped that she would be able to slip her cellphone to Casey if she could divert the intruder's attention long enough. He was so close that he was practically breathing down her neck. He reached out and groped her from behind saying, "You have a mighty fine ass. I wouldn't mind sampling what Mr. Famous Attorney has been dipping into." Laughing at his own comment, he asked, "Would you like to see how a real man takes his woman?"

Thinking fast, she decided to use any means available. "Actually, I know just what a man like you needs." Turning toward him slightly, she moved her hand to cup her own breast. "Do you want this?" she said suggestively, with bile rising up in her throat. "Let's make a deal. I give you my body and you let my friend go," Allie said.

"I can take you anytime I want, why would I bargain with you? I can have both of you. Maybe we should have a threesome. Hmm?"

Continuing with the twine, she tried reasoning, "Wouldn't it be much better to have me be a willing participant rather than just a wooden body you use and discard?" She added, "I know how to please a man like you. What harm would a trade like this do? Nobody has to know. Your boss will still be happy that you have me, and Casey gets to walk away."

She could tell he was becoming aroused, as his eyes darkened behind the mask. "You are very convincing *chica*. Beauty and brains, I like that," he said, leering as his eyes stripped her bare. "I can see that you want me. A sexy woman like you, I'm very tempted, but if I choose to take you up on your offer, I'll decide, and it will be on my terms. I take you if I want to and if I want your friend, well, I will take her, too. Finish tying up your friend and you and me will take a little break upstairs?" he said, as he grabbed Allie's breast squeezing, she winced in pain.

Allie tried to hide her revulsion. "That's not the deal. Do you want me warm and willing or not? I can pleasure you; I know how to please a man. I promise it will be worth it. In exchange, my friend will keep quiet, she won't tell a soul about this, and you let her go. She would do that to not risk my life. Right, Casey?" she encouraged her friend.

Casey nodded yes, with tears shimmering in her hazel eyes.

He considered her words, weakened by his obvious arousal. He said, "You will be my whore regardless. Upstairs now."

Allie had successfully distracted him long enough that he had lost focus on how she had secured the twine. She started to unbutton her blouse and moved toward him, making sure to keep him occupied. She dropped her phone to the ground and covertly tried kicking it toward Casey with her foot, while simultaneously reaching down to cup his erection and lightly squeeze. The ploy worked as he fell even further under her spell. He said in a strained voice, "You are mine." Grabbing her arm, he jerked her harshly dragging her towards the stairs.

"If you try to escape, your friend dies. Do you understand?" he said menacingly to Casey.

"Yes," Casey whispered.

"Good. I'm glad we understand each other. You wouldn't want to be responsible for what happens to your friend if you do something stupid. It will be slow and painful, I promise you," he said, smiling sadistically. "I would enjoy every minute of it. It's up to you."

Allie tried to communicate to Casey with her eyes, before being roughly pulled up the staircase and into the bedroom. He tore at her blouse, popping buttons as he ripped it from her body, leaving her exposed in just her lacey bra and jeans. He sat on the edge of the bed and demanded, "Now let's see you put on a show for me, take off your clothes."

Allie hesitated, and he snarled, "I'm not a patient man. Do you want to do this the hard way?" He began to rise from his seated position on the bed.

"No, just give me a moment." After slipping off her shoes, Allie slowly began to unzip her jeans, mustering every ounce of her dubious acting skills to play the role of her life. Slowly and seductively, she slid the jeans down her hips and thighs as he watched the show, practically drooling with unbridled anticipation, his piercing black eyes burning from beneath the mask. She stepped out of her jeans, leaving them in a pile on the floor.

He pointed his gun and said, "Now the bra and panties."

"What's the hurry? Let's take it slow." Allie tried stalling, desperately hoping that Casey was freeing herself and getting help. "Let me deliver on my promise," Allie said as she walked over to him and straddled his lap. She almost gagged from his body odor. Reaching up, she removed his mask and with inner revulsion pressed her lips to his, almost losing it when he thrust his tongue in her mouth. He groaned out loud and picked her up easily and tossed her onto the bed. Beside her on bended knees, he struggled to unbuckle his belt and unzip his own pants while holding the gun on her at the same time.

Allie lay sprawled out on the bed, praying that someone would get there soon. She was terrified, but even through her fear she strategized. Knowing he would be more vulnerable once his pants came off, she mentally prepared to take any opportunity that presented itself. He pulled his pants down to his knees and was struggling with his underwear as he crawled on top of her, his weight pinning her beneath him. As he forced his tongue into her mouth, she tried to turn her head away, only to have him grab her face and violently turn her back to his waiting lips. He grasped her hair and jerked it hard as he struck her across the face. She gasped in pain. She began to fight in earnest against his brutality. She kicked and pushed, trying to keep her legs tight together as he forced her thighs open wider while grabbing at her panties, the only barrier left between her and the unthinkable. Then, suddenly, he was no longer on top of her.

CHAPTER 22

She opened her eyes to see Zane holding onto the intruder's shirt with one hand as he pummeled his face with the other. The perpetrator was off balance, with his pants around his ankles, so Zane had the advantage. Because of the element of surprise, the gun had been forgotten where he had tucked it under the pillow. Allie was completely useless; her whole body was trembling with the aftershock of the attempted rape. The stranger suddenly head-butted Zane, then he dove for the bed, grabbing the gun he had left under the pillow. In a millisecond, he had his arm around Allie's throat and the gun pointed at her head. Zane stood back like a panther sizing up his prey.

"One move and I blow your *puta's* head off." He grinned maniacally. "Back out of the room now and close the door behind you."

Just then, Darcy stepped into the room with her gun pointed between his eyes. "Drop it *now*! You're outnumbered, and I'm an excellent shot. I will *not* miss," she threatened menacingly. "This house is surrounded. Give yourself up now and you'll only be charged with kidnapping and attempted rape. Put the gun down or I swear, if you live it will be to regret it."

Suddenly, he didn't look quite so smug. Instinctively, Allie emboldened by the extra support, sharply punched him in the groin, giving Zane and Darcy the opportunity they needed. Pouncing on him, Darcy wrestled the gun from his hand, while Zane pulled Allie into his arms.

"Pull up your pants, Asshole," Darcy said as she shoved him. He quickly did as she asked, fumbling with his zipper and belt buckle then Darcy slapped on handcuffs. She made him walk ahead as she followed with her gun trained on the back of his head.

"Allie," Zane said in a half-smothered sob into her hair. "I'm so sorry." He rocked her gently while she cried into his shoulder.

"I was so-so-so terrified," she stuttered, shaking with teeth chattering.

"Shh, I know. You're safe now. I'm going to let go for minute and grab a blanket to wrap around you."

"NO!" she said in panic. "No, don't let me go."

"Shh. It's okay, Allie. Take a few deep breaths. He's in custody now. He can no longer hurt you."

"Casey. Where is Casey? Is she alright?" she asked.

"Casey is fine. Just shook up, like you. Charlie is on his way, and the police are with her downstairs. I'm sure they're getting her statement right now." He struggled to reach for a blanket while holding her, so he wouldn't have to let her go. Finally succeeding, he wrapped it around her nakedness. Her breathing slowed and he could feel her starting to calm down, but she still clung to him like a frightened child.

He kissed her brow, making soothing noises as he continued to rock her.

~

When Allie was ready, Zane helped her get dressed and they went downstairs to see what they needed to do next. Allie ran over to Casey, and they just held each other and cried.

"You were so brave, Allie. Thank you," Casey said, overcome with emotion.

"What about you? You were right there with me Casey."

"But what *you* did was brilliant. We were doomed. If you hadn't been so quick-thinking, God knows what would have happened," Casey said.

"I was terrified," Allie admitted, "and completely winging it. I wasn't sure how he was going to react, but fortunately his brain was in his crotch, so it gained us some time."

"Oh, Allie, I just hope…," Casey said, trailing off.

Allie's voice trembled, "Zane and Darcy showed up just in time. Another couple of minutes and it would have been even more horrifying than it already was."

"I don't want you to talk about it now unless you need to. It's too soon, I just needed to know that he didn't … you know, rape you." Casey swallowed hard and began to sob. "Oh, Allie I was so terrified for you. I felt so helpless."

"Casey, I'll be okay. He didn't ... He almost ... I managed to...." Allie stumbled over her words, not able to articulate over the terror gripping her mind when she went back to that room. "Thank God they arrived when they did," she finished on a sob. "We were a team. It took both of us. You managed to get loose and make the call. You saved me," Allie reassured her friend.

Zane, taking charge, said, "They want us down at the station for your statement, Allie. We've got to go."

Zane was quiet and withdrawn on the way downtown, grappling with his own emotional storm, now that Allie was safe. He held her hand but didn't talk the entire ride to the precinct.

Upon their arrival, Allie was whisked away to a room to give her statement. Zane was put in another room to give his version of events. They offered her a beverage and she chose hot tea. She was still having tremors and the hot liquid felt soothing. She walked through the entire morning, ending with the attempted rape and subsequent rescue. Afterwards she joined Zane, and the detective explained to them both that they were able to match up the prints from the man in custody to the prints on the knife left behind Thanksgiving Day. They belonged to a small-time thug who was known as one of Duvall's men, who in turn worked for Santiago.

The detective said, "You're free to go, but I caution you that these are some pretty bad characters. Stay alert."

"We appreciate your service and we'll definitely be vigilant," Zane answered.

"We have to get you out of here. Casey and Charlie

offered their condo in Anna Maria Island, and it seems like a perfect place for you to hide out until this shit resolves. The company will put you on paid leave," he said.

"I don't want to leave you and Kit and everyone." Allie said.

"Casey and I talked about it, and she'll fly down with you to get settled," he said, brooking no argument. "She's making the reservations as we speak."

"Zane, I know this is impossibly hard for you too, but I don't want to feel isolated after what I just went through. Can't you understand? I need you."

Jaw clenched, he responded, "What I understand is that you're in danger, and for your best interests and mine, now is not the time to be sentimental and collapse into our emotions. We need to be sensible here. I don't need to fight you over every single decision. Why can't you just go along for once instead of arguing every time?" He knew he was doing what he said he didn't want to do—caving in to his own emotions and lashing out.

Allie unclasped her hand from his and jerked her head as if she had been slapped. "That is so unfair. If by arguing you mean having a say in my own life and decisions, then I guess I am guilty as charged," she said.

"Allie, I'm sorry. You know what I meant. I'm overwhelmed. I'm frightened for you. I'm in over my head. Just help me out here, just this once. Please?"

"I guess," she said.

"Did I hear right?" He grinned slightly, cupping his hand around his ear as if to amplify her words, attempting to lighten the air between them.

"Yes," she said, taking his hand in hers once again.

"Baby, that is music to my ears! You have no idea how much that means to me," he said, putting their clasped hands up to his lips and kissing the back of hers. His relief was immeasurable, and he could breathe for the first time in hours.

~

It was decided that the only way to keep Will and his family safe was to move them temporarily to a safe house. They were flown to Chicago and put up in a two-bedroom apartment in the city. It was a step above the motel room they had been existing in for the last two weeks.

The two older children ran around excitedly while the baby slept in his carrier. "Kids are so resilient," Will said wistfully.

"Thank God," Camilla responded. "Will, how long do you think we'll have to be here?" she asked.

"I have no idea. Your brother's trial date is coming up soon," he said.

"Why do you have to testify? Can't you just plead the fifth or something?" she asked naively.

"It's too late for that. Would you rather I go to prison for a crime your brother committed?" Will asked with frustration. "What do you expect from me?" he said, displaying anger at her for the first time since their nightmare began.

"I don't know, Will. I just know that if anything were to happen to my babies, I couldn't survive it."

"*Your* babies? They are *our* babies. And me? Could

you survive something happening to me?" he asked quietly.

"Of course not," Camilla said huffily. "Don't try to twist my words," she said, snapping at him, then immediately breaking down in tears.

Will immediately felt remorseful and pulled Camilla into his arms and held her until her tears subsided. "Cam," he said, brushing her hair back. "We'll get through this."

"My brother, though?" she said quietly.

"Camilla, this, all that has happened, is a result of his decisions. Not yours, not mine. He can burn in hell, as far as I'm concerned."

"I know you'll never be able to see the young and handsome boy who played with me in the poverty-stricken streets of Mexico, but I can never erase those memories."

"I'm not the monster here, Camilla. I'm trying to understand why you still feel any sense of loyalty to that sociopath. It's beyond my capabilities as a human being. I'm sorry that I'm failing you here, but I also feel that you're failing us. That boy you knew is dead. He's been replaced by a savage animal," Will said.

"I'm sorry you feel that way. I won't mention my brother to you again."

Sitting down next to her, he tried pulling her into his arms, but she stiffened in response to his touch. "Camilla, I know how much you love your brother. Darling, I love you and only want what is best for you and our children. Can't you see that? I know he is your brother, and I am sorry that he's betrayed you. I only know that I couldn't bear to lose you, or our babies, and

Christian is responsible for putting you all in harm's way. I don't know how to reach you. I don't want this to come between us on top of everything else. We should be a team here, us against the world. Instead, we're arguing with each other."

Softening, Camilla turned to Will and wrapped her arms around him, whispering into his shirt, her words muffled, *"Te amo y lo siento."*

She continued to cry softly as he rocked her in his arms. Will wanted to believe that her apology and assurance that she loved him meant that they were now on the same page about her brother. If not completely convinced, he acknowledged it was at least a start.

CHAPTER 23

*T*he last twenty-four hours had been a whirlwind leading up to this moment. She and Casey were cruising at thirty thousand feet over the earth on a two-and-a-half-hour flight to Sarasota-Bradenton International Airport. There, they would rent a car and drive to the condo, which was a beach-front property on Holmes Beach, Anna Maria Island.

Both women were emotionally spent and didn't talk much during the flight. Normally, Allie would have been excited for this visit. She and Jeff had spent several vacations with Casey and Charlie at their condo over their married years. Anna Maria Island still felt like old Florida. It had a quaint charm. You could ride bikes everywhere. There was great food, and the wide beach with soft white sand was one of the best kept secrets. She knew after settling in that it would be the perfect place to relax and heal from their trauma.

Casey planned on staying for ten days to get some

much-needed healing time for herself, and to support Allie after the ordeal she'd been through. There was nothing like hanging out on the beach with your bestie to get things back in perspective. The condo was a simple two-bedroom with quintessential beach décor. It was on the second floor, so they had a great view of the ocean. After unpacking their suitcases, they both sank down into the comfortable chairs on the balcony.

"I can't believe everything that's happened in the last forty-eight hours," Casey said.

"I know. Is this for real?" Allie asked. "What the hell. I'm still in shock. I'm trying to wrap my head around it all."

"I know, right?" Casey responded with her eyes closed. "Here we are sitting in shorts and tank tops, while a mere three hours ago we were in heavy parkas and there was snow on the ground. We may as well make the best of it since we're here. I for one, am going to pig out on seafood and bask in the sun and thank God we are safe and sound!"

"I'm so grateful, really I am, but I feel a little guilty," Allie admitted. "Leaving Zane to deal with that mess alone."

"He's far from alone. He has Darcy and the police department, three partners, Annika, Stella, the other lawyers at the firm, and we must not forget … Helen."

"Ha ha ha. You are so funny," Allie said, lightly punching her friend's arm.

"What do you want to do for dinner?" Casey asked.

"Well, I'm with you, when in Rome…," Allie said.

"Seafood it is." Casey smiled.

~

"Well, Kit Kat, it's you and me now." She jumped onto Zane's lap and began kneading his thighs before lying down and curling up. "Your mama won't be gone forever. She gets to laze around on the beach while we're stuck here with the bad guys and snow."

He randomly flipped through the television stations, trying to find a distraction. He decided on a college basketball game but watched it half-heartedly at best. His cell rang; he quickly answered, "Allie."

"Hi, is this Zane or Eeyore?" she laughed. "I'm calling to check in and let you know that we made it. The weather is perfect here, the sun's shining, and we're headed out for a seafood dinner. So why am I still miserable?" Allie said.

"I miss you too, Allie," he said.

"How's Kit?"

"Sitting curled up in my lap looking at me with her love lights on."

"That little tramp. No sense of loyalty." Allie complained.

"Well, I miss you enough for the both of us," he said.

"Honestly, I can't say I mind," Allie admitted.

"When this is all over, we're going to take a vacation together," Zane promised.

"Promise?"

"Promise."

"I've got to go; Casey is chomping at the bit."

"OK. Don't forget about me, Allie," Zane said.

"As if I could. I'll be in touch."

"Bye."

~

"*W*hat, no 'I love you'?" Casey asked.

"Nope. I made that mistake once and felt utterly humiliated. I know Zane has feelings for me, I just don't know how deep they are. His ex-wife still has designs on him and I'm just not sure he isn't still holding on to something for her as well. He's loaning Helen his lake house while her house is being remodeled. That's a little suspect to me," Allie said.

"Maybe not. They were married, after all. There's nothing to say you can't have some sort of a relationship with an ex," Casey said.

"Yeah," Allie answered, "but their divorce was so dirty I can't imagine why he'd want to have anything to do with her."

"Maybe he doesn't. Maybe he's just a nice guy who has a hard time saying no to someone he once cared about," Casey said.

"You could be right, but it just seems a little strange to me. Anyway, let's go eat," Allie said.

They decided to walk since it was such a beautiful evening, and they greeted other travelers and locals as they strolled along. Both women were already beginning to relax. Allie was thankful that Zane had insisted she take this time away.

They arrived at the restaurant and were seated immediately. The ambiance was casual, as were most places on Anna Maria Island. That Southern, laid-back vibe was just what they needed, Allie thought, as she glanced around.

On the way back to the condo they took a short stroll on the beach. The sound of the ocean waves moving in and out in their mysterious timeless rhythm comforted Allie. It reminded her that her life was just a blink of the eye. This would pass. The sun would rise and set, and the waves would continue to churn and roll in and out.

The stars were bright in the sky, which reminded her of her night at the lake with Zane, after they had returned from boating and of what had followed. She almost blushed thinking about how erotic it had been. She knew that Zane had stolen her heart. She was in love with him. She didn't know anything beyond that simple, irrefutable fact, but she didn't need to. The future would take care of itself. The ocean reminded her that she had no control anyway.

CHAPTER 24

*A*llie dropped Casey off at the airport reluctantly. The time had flown by. They both cried as they said their goodbyes. "Just use this time to heal," Casey said. "We don't get many opportunities in our adult lives to just chill. I loved spending this time together, even under these circumstances," she said warmly. "It's been a long time since we've had a girl's trip."

"Yes, and let's not wait so long for the next one," Allie said.

She watched as Casey walked through the first security checkpoint and turned to wave at her. She waited until Casey disappeared around the corner before leaving. She decided to return to the condo, change into her swimsuit, and read a novel on the beach.

Grabbing a beach towel, sunglasses, and bottle of water, she slipped into her flip-flops and headed for the sun and sand. Allie chose a section of the beach that was secluded and away from other vacationers who were taking advantage of this beautiful sunny day. She laid out her beach towel and settled face down, with her cheek nestled on bent arms.

The ocean waters were calm, and the warm breeze caressed Allie's skin. She closed her eyes, taking in the sounds of the gulls and the waves lapping at the shore. She could hear children's laughter off in the distance, probably the same kids she had noticed making a sandcastle. Lost in the moment, she became drowsy and eventually drifted off into a light sleep. She was startled awake by someone plopping down beside her. She awoke in a slight panic and pushed herself up quickly.

"Zane. What are you doing here?" she said, placing a hand on her heart.

"Hi, Baby," he said, leaning over to plant a kiss on her surprised open mouth. The passion ignited immediately. Allie reached out to touch his broad muscular shoulders and to run her fingers through the soft, dark hair on his chest.

"Are you really here? I'm not dreaming, am I?" she asked in a daze, caressing his face and running her fingers through his thick hair.

"No, Babe, I'm here in flesh and blood," he said. He could barely keep his hands off her. He leaned in for a deep kiss, his arousal apparent through the large bulge in his trunks. "I'm only here for the weekend, but Casey and I coordinated schedules so that I would arrive and surprise you the day she left."

Tears shimmered in her eyes, "I don't know what to say. This is the best surprise I've ever had."

"It's a good thing I decided to come. It should be against the law for you to be out in public in that swimsuit. I can't bear to think of other men ogling my woman."

"What about you? You look like a Greek god with those six-pack abs and those two dimples just above your yummy butt. I can see all the women drooling, and I'm the lucky girl who gets to touch." She reached for his head to pull him back in for a deep kiss.

"I vote we return to the condo and let me show you how lucky you are," Zane said.

"Deal."

He stood and reached down to take Allie's hand. They gathered their beach items and started back to the condo. Zane intentionally hanging back a bit so he could watch her sexy body as she walked ahead.

"My God, Allie, your ass. Am I really the guy that gets to lay with you tonight?"

"Only if you promise to ravish me thoroughly," she replied.

"No objections from me."

They entered the condo and, as soon as the door closed, they were in each other's arms. Zane wanted to devour her. He felt like his thirst could never be quenched. He released the tie of her swimsuit top and removed it, letting it drop to the floor. His breath caught in his throat as he studied her ripe breasts and pink nipples erect from arousal, with a faint tan line where they had been protected from the sun. With his arms wrapped around her, he slid both hands down her back, reaching under her tiny bikini bottoms to grope and knead her buttocks. He reached between them with one hand to insert his finger into the delicate wet spot between her legs. Allie moaned loudly.

"Zane, I've missed you. I need you; I want to feel you inside of me."

He picked her up in his arms, carried her to the bedroom, and laid her on the bed. Her face was flushed with desire, her eyes dazed with lust, which aroused him to a fever pitch. He tore at his own swim trunks, dragging them down over his full erection.

Seeing him standing naked before her, his masculinity in full display, she pleaded, "Now, Zane," with an urgency that matched his. Suddenly he was on top of her, plunging into her moistness, riding her hard and fast, both of them climaxing quickly.

Afterwards, as they lay panting in each other's arms, he began to kiss her from her head to her toes. "I love that tiny mole right here," he said, kissing her on the swell of her breast. As he kissed his way down her body, he stopped to linger between her legs, causing Allie to shiver with delight. When he reached her feet, he rolled her onto her stomach and began to kiss his way back up, kissing the sensitive spots behind her knees and on up to the buttocks and back.

When he reached her neck, he slowly moved his hardness between her thighs and parted her legs wide with his knees. With Allie still lying on her belly, Zane held his own weight with an arm on either side of her, his fingers interlaced with hers. His back flexed and his biceps and triceps bulged as he supported his own weight. He stroked between her legs with his hardness. Allie groaned as the friction caused her arousal to build again. He smoothly rolled her onto her side and thrust into her vagina from behind, pumping wildly as he squeezed her nipple with one hand while fingering her clit with the other before exploding in orgasm. Allie followed right behind, climaxing as she yelled out his name.

He spooned her tightly against him, cupping her breasts as he nuzzled her neck. He whispered so low she strained to hear, "I love you, Allie." Afraid to move or respond, afraid she had only imagined it, she lay still.

After their lovemaking, they slept for several hours, naked limbs intertwined, content to be held in one another's arms. When Allie awoke, she climbed out of bed trying not to disturb Zane, who was still snoozing. She pulled on a lightweight silk robe and cinched the belt around her waist.

After grabbing a bottle of water, she went out to the balcony and sat down, propping her legs up on an ottoman. She needed a moment alone to absorb what had transpired between herself and Zane. That he had made the time and effort to fly down for the weekend opened her heart to hope. She still questioned whether she had heard him declare his love for her or if it had been wishful thinking on her part.

She let the sound of the ocean waves transport her, trying to forget about everything but this moment. She would savor this time here with Zane because no one knew what the future held or when they would see each other again.

After some time had passed, as the sun was setting, Zane joined her on the balcony. He chose to sit on the ottoman, placing Allie's feet in his lap so he could massage them. His strong, capable hands stretched each toe one at a time and then, using his thumbs, he gently probed into the soft soles of her feet. As he kneaded and twisted with a gentle grip, Allie surrendered to the sensations. "If you ever decide to give up on law, you certainly could have a second career as a reflexologist," Allie murmured, so relaxed it felt like an effort to speak.

"So I've been told." Teasing, he winked at her.

"You had better watch what you say, since you're currently pretty vulnerable, with my feet a mere inch from your crotch," she threatened and nudged him gently with her toes to prove the point.

"Hey, whoa," he protested. "I may have use for that later." Zane raised his eyebrows suggestively.

"Don't be so sure of yourself," Allie said

"I'm only going by your body and it's response to my awesome love making skills. Nothing pleases me more than pleasing you, my love." He said it so casually that Allie blinked at him like an owl.

"What?" Zane asked in response to her wide-eyed stare.

"Nothing," she answered quickly, not wanting to spoil the moment with words.

He placed her feet back on the ottoman and, straddling her legs, leaned down to kiss her on the tip of her nose. "Don't look so surprised. You must know by now that I am completely, utterly, captivated by you. I love you Allie Mae Rose." He tilted her head up to look deep into her eyes, "Now, since I know how much you like to eat, let's shower, get dressed, and find some good seafood," he said.

"Well, I guess you really do know me. You just read my mind, Mr. Dunn," Allie replied, smiling as she rose gracefully from the chair to follow him inside.

～

*R*eturning from dinner with full bellies, they sprawled out on the couch to watch a little TV before retiring for the evening. Zane paused with the remote in his hand, uncharacteristically hesitant with his words.

"Allie, earlier, when I first arrived, I felt so happy to see you that I kind of got carried away by the moment." He continued, "I hope that I didn't move too fast, considering what you just went through. As a man, I'm left to my imagination about how frightening that experience must have been for you, and, frankly, I'm almost ashamed to be a man. It felt right in the moment, but, in hindsight, I hope it wasn't too soon for you." His voice was serious and heavy with self-doubt.

"Zane, I needed that. Making love to you, well, I don't know quite how to explain it, and everyone is different, but for me I needed it to replace that awful memory. Your beautiful lovemaking is healing for me. It is like a balm to my soul. Your concern touches me deeply. Thank you for that."

"When I think of what could have happened to you, I almost lose my mind!" Zane said.

"Coming here to Florida was a perfect plan. First Casey, then you, showing up to take care of me. I feel so loved and supported and most of all safe. That means the world to me, Zane. I'm going to be okay." Allie nestled her head into the crook of his arm and cuddled up with his arms around her. He leaned in for a chaste kiss and turned on the television, tuning in to a light comedy. They both fell asleep and stayed huddled there for the rest of the night.

CHAPTER 25

All too soon Sunday arrived, and it was almost time for Zane to leave for the airport. Sniffling, she said, "I don't want you to go."

"Believe me, I'd rather be here with you than anywhere in the world, but unfortunately reality has a way of intruding on my desires," he said.

"I know. I don't have to like it though."

"Go ahead and wallow—it makes me feel wanted."

"I'm not wallowing," she said. "Well, maybe just a little."

"I have a surprise for you, Allie."

"Another surprise?"

"Yes, but you'll have to wait until later to find out what it is," he replied mysteriously. "Just keep that in mind rather than focusing on me leaving, okay? I promise you'll love this surprise,"

Looking at his watch, he said, "I've got to get to the

airport and my taxi is here. Be good. Why don't you buy yourself a muumuu and throw away that horrible bikini you own?" he grinned. "It just isn't your color."

Allie laughed, watching her gorgeous man walk away, and said, "I'll think about it. Bye, be careful." He saluted her and hopped into the cab.

Allie waved until she could no longer see the taxi, then walked slowly back to her condo.

Slipping on athletic shoes, loose-fitting shorts and a tank top, she headed for the beach. Jogging along parallel to the lapping waves, she quickly found her rhythm and gait, breath steady and sure. She became immersed in the runner's zone.

She passed sandpipers running towards and away from the waves, seemingly in an endless game of tag with the water's edge. There were countless pelicans diving like torpedoes into the ocean for the catch of the day. She noticed three dolphins fairly close to shore, almost as if they were swimming alongside with her. She jogged by children with buckets and shovels playing in the sand, families sitting under bright umbrellas, young teenagers sunning themselves, a man throwing a Frisbee to his big Lab. Passing a man with a pole stuck in the sand and his long fishing line in the water, she stopped to catch her breath and head home.

"Catching anything?" Allie asked.

His face was lined and weathered from many years in the sun. He looked like he was completely in his element, one with the sea. He was slightly stooped and wore old and faded cargo shorts and a T-shirt with a local fish market's logo. "I've had a pretty good day so far. I've caught some snapper and redfish. Been a productive afternoon," he said smiling.

"Are you from here?" she asked.

"Born and raised," he replied. "Must have done something right in a past life."

"Yes, I'd have to agree. This is pretty much paradise," Allie said, smiling warmly.

"I'm Allie," she said, offering her hand.

After scrubbing his hands against his cargo shorts, he reached for her proffered hand. "Ray. A pleasure to meet you, Allie." He smiled. "There's live music tonight at the Island Time Bar and Grill. Me and a few old cronies play some light jazz during dinner hour, if you're interested."

"I know that place. My friend and I dined there the other evening. That sounds perfect," Allie smiled. "I knew I stopped here for a reason. That's just what I need. What time do you start playing?" she asked.

"From five to nine o'clock, with a half-hour break in there," he said.

"Great. See you later," she promised, stretching out her quads and hamstrings for her return jog back. "Bye, and thanks for the invite." She headed back to the condo, having successfully shaken off her melancholy mood.

～

*A*llie was dressing for dinner when she heard a knock at the door. Thinking it might be her "surprise"—flowers maybe—she smiled as she went to answer, but she paused before opening to call, "Who is it?"

"Open up." A voice sounding uncannily like her mother's, responded.

"Mom?" Allie said through the closed door.

"Yes, Dear, it's your mother."

Allie unlocked the deadbolt and swung the door wide. Sarah and Pete stood there with big, satisfied grins on their faces. "Mom!" Allie said with a sob, rushing to throw her arms around her. "What ... how ... when ... What's going on?" she finally managed to squeak out.

"Oh, Sweetie, we've been so worried about you, and Casey and Zane came up with the idea that we could all tag team to help you settle in and get comfortable. That Zane is really something. You'd better hang on to that one," Sarah said matter-of-factly. "Pete and I drove down. We took our time and stopped to visit a few places we had always wanted to see on our way here. Last night, we stayed in Savannah, Georgia. Loved it." she exclaimed. "Pete, we loved it didn't we?" she asked him, pulling his hand so he would be included.

"Yes, we sure did, Sarah," Pete said, looking at her mom with adoration. He had such lovely and kind eyes, Allie thought. Laugh lines fanned out from light blue eyes framed by thick dark lashes. A thick mop of once-dark curly hair, most of which had turned gray, and dark brows highlighted his features. He was in very good shape and quite handsome. She could see why her mom was interested.

"Well, how long are you staying?" Allie asked.

"We can only stay for a few days before we have to head back. Pete has some appointments he has to keep and, with the holidays around the corner, all his children and grandchildren will be flying in," Sarah said.

"I am so happy to see you both," Allie said beaming. "I'll take what I can get. I was just heading out for dinner. I met a fisherman on the beach today who plays in a jazz group, and he invited me to pop in to listen. Do you guys have any interest?" she asked.

"We deliberately didn't eat so we could have dinner together. We'll be ready to go once we unload our suitcases," Sarah said.

"I'll go down and get them now," Pete said.

"I'll help you," Allie volunteered.

"No, I've got it. You visit with your Mom. I'll be right back," he said kindly.

Once the door closed behind Pete, Allie pulled Sarah onto the balcony and sat her down on a chair while Allie rested on the ground at her feet. She immediately began quizzing her. "When did you leave? What car did you drive? Where else did you go?" She rattled on without waiting for an answer.

Sarah's forehead creased, "Darling, let's discuss all that at dinner. What I want to know is, how are you holding up?"

"I'm hanging in there, "Allie said, laying her head on her mother's lap. Sarah gently smoothed Allie's hair back from her brow. "If I stay in the moment, I'm okay, but if I get ahead of myself or think back to recent events, I freak out a little," Allie admitted.

"That's completely understandable, Honey. You've

been through quite an ordeal." Sarah said soothingly. "I'm always available, any time you need to talk."

"I know that, Mom. I still can't believe Zane was here and now he's gone. I'm shocked at how much I miss him."

"Well if you want to open your heart to love, that just goes with the territory," Sarah said. "Zane is a good man. I think it's safe to trust your gut on this one. I don't think he's the type to lead someone on if he's not really interested. He seems like an all-in kind of guy. But I'm not the one living your life."

"It's too late anyway. I love him." Allie sighed.

Pete stuck his head out on the balcony to inform them that he was finished unloading their luggage, so they set off for the restaurant on foot. The Island Time Bar and Grill was an open-air bar with a patio and had a laid-back island vibe. Allie waved to Ray the fisherman, who was playing the upright bass on stage. He nodded and smiled at her as they were seated. They put in an order for the raw bar sampler as an appetizer and decided to get a pitcher of margaritas to share. They went ahead and placed their dinner order at the same time since they were all so hungry.

"Casey had the coconut shrimp when we were here and loved it," Allie shared. "I think I'm going to order the fish-n-chips."

"They both sound good, but I think I'll have the shrimp quesadilla," Sarah said. "I'll add some guacamole and chips. Would you want to split the quesadilla and guac and chips, Pete?".

"Sure, that sounds like a good idea. With the apps, that should be plenty of food," he replied.

Allie had only had a sip of her margarita when her stomach suddenly started to feel a slight bit queasy. Their food arrived, and Allie barely picked at her meal, causing her mom to express concern. "What's wrong, Honey, you are barely touching your meal? That's so not like you," she commented.

"I don't know. I suddenly started to feel nauseous," Allie said. "I'm sure it's all the stress I've been under," she said reassuringly. "How do you both like your food?"

"Very tasty," Sarah said.

"Delicious," Pete said. "These margaritas are really good, too."

After they had finished their meals, the band started playing an old Herb Alpert song, "This Guy's in Love with You." Pete asked Sarah to dance. Allie so wished Casey were here so they could nudge each other and enjoy this moment of seeing her mom being led around the dance floor. It was so romantic. She pulled out her cellphone and covertly snapped a photo of the two of them to text to Casey. They looked so good together, and it seemed as if love was blossoming between them. It made her miss Zane in the worst way.

Walking home later, Sarah and Pete were hand-in-hand with Allie's arm looped through her mom's. Allie thought that it had been a lovely evening to remember. She was grateful to have time to get to know Pete a little better. She found herself liking him a lot. He was good for her mom.

Back at the condo, they all agreed that it was time for bed, so they said their goodnights and headed to their respective bedrooms. Brushing her teeth after flossing, Allie reviewed the last week, thinking of all the love she had in her life. She felt so lucky. As she crawled between the sheets, her last thought before she switched off the lamp was of Zane—raw, powerful, and naked. With a smile, she slipped into a deep sleep.

CHAPTER 26

Zane had been back from Florida for about a week and, although Annika was more than competent, she wasn't Allie. He missed her. He knew he was back to his old, pre-Allie impatience. He didn't like the way the office seemed to be tiptoeing around him, but he felt incapable of self-correction. Allie had a way of bringing out the best in him. He liked himself a whole lot better when she was around. *Oh well, today's a whole new day.* No time like the present to get on the right track.

While sitting at his desk, a call came in from Helen, which without thinking he automatically picked up. "Hello," Zane said.

"Zane, darling, I need you to come to the lake house as soon as possible," she said. Somehow everything that came out of her mouth always sounded seductive.

"Um let's see…that would be a no. Helen, I'm slammed here at work, I don't have time for your games. What seems to be the problem?" Zane asked, not really wanting to know the answer, but ingrained habits of courtesy died hard.

"Darling, it appears that there have been vandals here. When I went out to the garage a few minutes ago, the place had been ransacked. You need to come and see if anything is missing and to fill out a report for your insurance and the police, who have been called," she said.

"Wait, what?" he said, coming to attention since it wasn't just Helen's normal spoiled, childish request, which he usually tuned out.

"Weren't you listening?" she asked peevishly. "I said that someone broke into your garage and vandalized it. It is utter chaos. Only you can tell if anything is missing, and the police need to fill out a report. You must come immediately," she commanded.

"Dammit," he said with frustration. "Have you contacted the police yet?" he asked.

"I just told you that I already called the police and they need to speak to you," she said with exasperation.

"I'll see what I can do. I have a few loose ends to tie up here and then I'll get on the road. It's a five-hour drive, as you know, so don't expect me before six," he said impatiently.

"Thank you, my love. I'll be waiting." And she hung up on him before he could respond.

Zane was beyond frustrated with this latest calamity. There weren't enough hours in the day to begin with, and, although he wouldn't trade it for the world, the time in Florida had set him back. He called Annika into his office and explained the situation and that he would be out for the rest of the day and probably most of the following day as well. He gave her a list of things she could work on while he was away, then packing his briefcase headed out the door. He stopped by Stella's desk and briefly filled her in as well.

Zane drove straight through without stopping and arrived shortly after six o'clock. He was tired and grumpy as he grabbed his bag and briefcase and walked in the door. Helen greeted him with a glass of wine already poured and soft music playing on the record player. She was wearing a casual yet seductive, body-hugging straight black dress with a V neckline open to the waist in the front and back. She wore a wide silver belt. Her shimmering black hair was worn down, cascading around her shoulders.

"Hello, Zane," she said. "I've missed you."

"Hello, Helen," he said, sighing as he set his bags down and raked his hands through his hair.

"I'll wait on the wine, thanks. I'm going out to the garage to evaluate the damage," he said.

"Let me get my coat and I'll join you."

"I'm sure I can figure it out, Helen," he snapped.

"Zane," she said pouting, "there's no need to take your frustration out on me. You should be grateful I was staying here. God knows how long it might have taken you to discover it on your own." She was always good at taking credit whenever possible.

"Yes, Helen, you're right. Thank you for taking care of this. Now, let me get out there to see what, if anything, is missing. Just stay put. I'll be back in a bit," he said with exaggerated patience.

Coyly looking up through her thick eyelashes, she replied, "Whatever you say, Zane."

Entering the garage, he looked around, wondering where to start. Everything that had been stored on shelves was strewn around the garage floor. The metal storage cabinets, the same. Doing a mental inventory of garden and lawn tools and equipment, nothing appeared to be missing. He had a momentary suspicion that Stella herself was capable of this level of duplicity, then shrugged it off and concentrated on figuring out if anything was taken. His best guess would be teenagers out getting into trouble...vandalism for the hell of it. He would start organizing and putting things away in the morning and file the police report afterward.

When he returned inside, Helen had set the table and there were lit candles in the center. There was a bottle of wine in the cooler and two glasses already poured. He could smell garlic and realized that he was very hungry, since he had skipped lunch.

"Smells great," he said appreciatively.

"It's your favorite—steak paprika and garlic mashed potatoes," Helen said. "Come, have a seat. It's almost ready."

"Let me go wash my hands and throw my things in a bedroom and I'll be right back." Making his exit, he took the guest room Allie had used. When he returned, his plate was already on the table, with the steak in wine and heavy cream sauce served over the potatoes and asparagus on the side.

"This looks and smells delicious," Zane said. "Thanks."

"I had forgotten how much I like this house," Helen said.

"You didn't when we were married," Zane said dryly.

"Please don't start sniping at me," she replied. "I miss us, Zane. Remember when we met in the constitutional law class our first semester of law school?" she said nostalgically. "You walked in, and I was bowled over."

"Yes, of course I remember. You weren't too bad yourself," Zane said. "What was it, about a week into classes, and we were already an item? We didn't waste any time. Ah youth, to be young and dumb again."

"You were and are the sexiest man I had ever set eyes on," she said. "After being in an all-girl's private high school and then a women's college for my four years of undergraduate school, I was a bit sheltered at twenty-three."

"I would have never known it, the way you came on to me," he said.

"I said sheltered, not shy," Helen said then laughed. "Remember how hard my family was on you the first time you came home to meet them? You know Daddy. Nothing was ever good enough for his perfect daughter."

Helen had grown up in a very wealthy family, and it was old money, generations of old money. Her father was a very powerful attorney who had made his name representing the richest families of Chicago. He felt entitled to anything he desired and had passed that on to his only child.

"Zane, we were happy once. I know I made a mistake by taking a lover, but you were never around. I was so young when we got together. I didn't have much experience, it just happened." She excused herself like it was a minor infraction that he was being unreasonable about.

"Helen, you had a three-year affair behind my back that only ended because you got caught. I was the unlucky schmuck to discover you in our bed," he said, still remembering the hurt of the betrayal.

"I've changed, Zane. I now realize how stupid I was. You loved me once, can't you possibly rekindle that love again? There was never anyone for me but you. That affair was purely about sex. I never loved Duncan, it's you that I love." She reached for his hand; her long, manicured nails painted a bright red that matched her dramatic red lip color. Standing, she leaned over and pressed her lips against Zane's.

Zane pulled back and gently said, "Helen, I will always care about you. We were married for ten years, but I'm no longer in love with you. That chapter of our lives is over. You must know that."

Her jaw clenched. "It's because of that blonde groupie that was in your office, isn't it? I knew it."

"No, it's not because of Allie, but I am in love with her," he said kindly.

"Zane, Zane, Zane, she is much too insipid. You need someone who is as powerful as you are. She is weak." Helen continued, oblivious to Zane's darkening expression, "You need a mate, not a doormat. I am your equal, she is most definitely not. She is beautiful, I will give you that...but that isn't enough to hold your interest for long."

"You're mistaking power for control. Allie is not only empowered, she is highly intelligent, compassionate, funny, and sexy as hell," Zane said. "You, on the other hand, are not happy unless you are controlling everything and everyone around you. You will use any means to win and get what you want. That is not true power, Helen."

He continued, "I'm not worthy of Allie, but I'm a much better person when I'm with her than when I'm not. She makes me want to be a better person. She attracts what she wants and needs *to* her, because she is a generous and kind person. She doesn't have to resort to manipulation and deceit." He finished his angry defense and laid down his sword. "I don't want to fight with you, Helen. We shared a moment in time together. We had some great years in there. It just wasn't a forever kind of love."

"Oh, and now you're the expert? You think she is the 'forever kind of love'? Ha. Don't fool yourself. You will tire of her. You need fire. You will be bored in six months. Mark my words." She practically spit the words out.

"Helen, you're not the scorned woman here. Relax. We're divorced, remember? You've had a few relationships since then. Not that it's any of your business, but Allie is the least boring person I have ever met. I hate to break it to you, but emotional drama does not equate to excitement. Fighting and constant drama bore me to tears, and that is what our relationship was all about. Just let it go, Helen. Let's remember the good times and move on. Friends?" he asked, holding out his hand to shake on it.

Completely ignoring his outstretched hand, she replied, "I'm not giving up entirely. We will wait and see how you feel in a few months, Darling. I predict you will see the light and come crawling back to me. You know how good our sex life was. Are you sure you don't want to have a romp tonight, for old time's sake?"

"You are persistent, I will give you that, Helen." Zane laughed cynically. "Thanks for the lovely meal. I give it a five-star review. Now, I'm going to load the dishwasher then turn in and do a little work from my bedroom. I'm behind the eight ball right now. I'll see you in the morning. I plan to get an early start. I'll be up by six o'clock to reorganize the garage and then I'll drive over to the police precinct to fill out a report. I'll take off from there."

Zane rose and started to clean up. Helen haughtily left the room, presumably to sulk in her bedroom.

CHAPTER 27

Zane had left his cellphone plugged in to his charger on the kitchen counter when it rang. Without hesitation, Helen answered it with a sultry voice. "Hello," she said.

"Oh, um, this is Allie. Is Zane there?" she inquired tentatively. "Is this Helen?" she then asked in shock.

"Who else would it be, Allie? Zane is in the shower. Can I tell him you called?" Helen said with a falsely sweet voice. "We're here at the lake house. Thank God most of the snow missed us, so we aren't completely snowed in," she said. "Although that might not be such a bad thing. I'm sure we could find many ways to entertain ourselves." she said conspiratorially.

"Um, no, please don't bother telling him I rang. It wasn't important. I will try him again later. Thanks then. Uh, have a good time, Helen," Allie said, holding back tears.

"Oh, don't worry darling, we intend to. Bye now."

And she hung up on Allie smiling like the cat who swallowed the canary.

Allie hung up the phone and sat staring at the wall in shock. To say she felt devastated was an understatement. What was Zane doing at the lake house with Helen? In her opinion, there were no reasonable explanations. She could not come up with any good explanation for him to be there showering in the same house as his ex-wife. The betrayal was a visceral feeling deep in her gut. She protectively cupped her belly.

∼

Zane finished with the garage in less than an hour and, after filing the report with the police, headed back home. Helen had been in an extremely good mood when she had said her goodbyes. *Go figure.* He would never understand that woman and was glad to not have to spend all that energy trying anymore. She had wrapped her arms around his neck and tried to kiss him on the lips, but he had given her his cheek and hugged her briefly before climbing behind the wheel of his SUV and taking his leave.

That was odd, Zane thought to himself. He had left several messages for Allie this morning and no return call. He was beginning to be concerned. This last message he left had expressed an urgency and that if he didn't hear from her soon, he would be contacting the local police department to check on her. Several minutes later his phone rang, and it was Casey.

The minute Zane said hello, Casey immediately started chastising him. "How could you? Allie opened her heart, and this is all it meant to you? I am shocked. I thought you were a better person than this."

"Whoa. Wait a minute, what the hell are you talking about?" Zane said.

"What were you doing at the lake house with Helen at 7:00 this morning taking a shower?"

"What? Oh, that. How did you know that I was at the lake with Helen anyway?"

"Allie called you this morning, and Helen answered your phone and told her you were in the shower and implied that you were enjoying much more than you should be, considering your relationship with Allie. But maybe we have all misunderstood your real intentions here," Casey said.

"Casey, you have to believe me when I say that I would never in a million years have an intimate relationship with Helen again, even if it meant celibacy for the rest of my life."

"Tell that to Allie, who is sitting in her condo right now crying her eyes out,"

"I'm in love with Allie. She's it for me. I'm a one-woman kind of guy. I always have been. I'm not a player. Surely you believe that. It must look bad from your perspective, but I'm innocent. Helen was just being her normal devious self to imply that there was anything more to it. No wonder she seemed so pleased with herself when I left. I should have known something was up. I went there because she called to tell me that there had been some vandalism, which needed my attention. She was telling the truth about that. I drove down, had dinner, went to bed, got up early, dealt with the mess, filed a report, and left immediately," he explained.

Relenting, Casey said, "Well, I will give Allie a ring and tell her to pick up your call. She is pretty devastated. It is hard for her to completely trust someone after having her husband cheat on her. That does something to a person's soul. You have to give her a little slack for jumping to the worst conclusion. Helen was pretty convincing."

"Oh, I'm sure she was. She should have gone into acting instead of law," he said with jaw clenched. "I will deal with her later. For now, please call Allie and pave the way for me, OK? And thanks, Casey, you're a great friend to Allie and, therefore, my friend as well," he said sincerely.

"I'll call her, but she is pretty upset. Hopefully she'll take your call. I'll do my best," Casey said. "I'm sure she'll come around. If she doesn't pick up the first time, keep trying."

❧

"How do you know he was telling the truth?" Allie argued with Casey.

"You have to trust me. I have a good instinct for sniffing out liars. He was shocked, and I know he was telling me the truth. It all makes sense, and you know what a viper Helen is. I know it's hard for you, but Zane deserves a chance to explain.

"I'll think about it. I just need a little time," Allie said.

"Well, don't take too much time," Casey said.

Allie promised to think about it and signed off.

After several hours and ten missed phone calls, Allie relented and picked up on the next call. "Hello," She said.

"Allie, for God's sake, what kind of man do you think I am?" Zane said with exasperation. "Do you think I'm the type of man to go around telling all the women I date that I am in love with them? Allie, believe me, nothing happened with Helen. I told her that I was in love with you," he said.

"You really told her that?" Allie asked, still a bit sulky.

"Yes. She wasn't happy about it, which is why she pulled this stunt with answering my phone when you called, which I intend to deal with later."

"I guess I was quick to judge, and I apologize for that. You know my history and I'm just so vulnerable right now. I have a hard time trusting. But I do believe you. Really, I do. I'm really sorry."

"I know how convincing Helen can be. Trust me on that, I was married to her for ten years. But I love you and only you," Zane said. "I wish I could hop on a plane and fly down there immediately, but that's not an option. I hope you understand."

"Of course. Stay focused. We can talk by phone and hopefully this will all be over soon. I love you too."

CHAPTER 28

The Windy City lived up to its name. Will had bundled up in layers with a scarf, hat, and gloves as well as his thick parka, and the chill wind still penetrated his clothing as he returned to the apartment loaded down with enough groceries to last several days.

There were a lot of people walking about downtown this time of year. The holidays were fast approaching, and he and his family had settled in nicely. At times, they felt a little stir crazy from being cooped up, but they tried to get out at least once every day. They had decorated the apartment for Christmas, for the children's sake, and were able to buy a few toys for each of them to place under the small artificial tree they had put up.

Daniel and Isabella were excited that Santa was coming and had watched *Rudolph the Red-Nosed Reindeer* several times already. Their joy and innocence were contagious. You couldn't help but see it in their bright and shining eyes. Sometimes, he could almost convince himself that things were normal. He and Camilla were getting along, and the kids as always played well together and lavished attention on the baby.

Even so, the constant fear that gnawed at him could not be assuaged. The trial couldn't get here soon enough. Zane assured him that it would all be over soon. He prayed Zane was right. He hoped they could resume a normal life at some point in the future. As he approached the high-rise, he noticed two suspicious-looking men at about the exact moment they spotted him. He threw down his packages, turned and ran as fast as he could.

He shoved past people, accidently knocking some off balance as he pushed through the pedestrians. Though the crowd slowed him down, it was also great cover for him to make a getaway. He had the advantage of having spotted them from a distance, so he was already ahead by quite a bit. He knew the train station was about two miles away. If he could make it there, he could get lost more easily and hopefully locate Amtrak police officers and security. He had to get a warning to Camilla as soon as he could. If he could duck into the station, maybe he would be able to phone her from his cell. He couldn't chance slowing down now.

Risking a quick look behind him, he didn't see anyone on his tail, but he was sure they were there somewhere. He was almost to Union Station and the stairs were right before him. He took them two at a time, then he heard a shot ring out. Someone was firing at him. He managed to push through the doors and enter the station, with adrenalin surging through his

body. He franticly looked around, making a split decision to head for the boarding gates and waiting areas.
They were packed with travelers, and he tried to slow
down and blend in. He took off his coat, hat, and scarf
and quickly stuffed them in a trash receptacle.

Spotting a souvenir shop, he ducked inside and
grabbed a Chicago Cubs baseball cap and Cubs bomber
jacket from the rack. He then added a pair of reading
glasses he spotted on his way to check out. Tearing off
the tag from the hat, he stuck it on his head before
paying. Donning the glasses after peeling off the sticker
on the lens and ripping the tag with his teeth, he waited
nervously in line.

Furtively, he watched to see if he had been made, so
far, he was secure. As he stepped up to pay, he saw two
men rushing by outside the store and kept his head
down low. They ran by, scrutinizing the shoppers
surrounding him and they moved on, seeming to have
missed him with his change of attire. He took a deep,
steadying breath trying to calm himself down, so he
could think rationally and strategically.

Quickly leaving after paying for his purchases, he
turned, pulled on the jacket, and headed in the opposite
direction he had seen the men running. Sprinting to the
nearest Quik-Trak Kiosk, he purchased a ticket for the
train to Toledo, which was leaving in fifteen minutes.
He got in line at the boarding gate, trying to blend in
with the other travelers.

As he was checking in with the attendant and
entering the concourse where the train departed, they
spotted him, and his cover was blown. The two men
frantically looked around for a kiosk stand to

purchase tickets, so they could enter the departure area. Will pushed his way past the people in front of him and began to run alongside the platform as fast as he could, parallel to the waiting trains and empty tracks. He found his train and jumped on, quickly rushing to the nearest restroom and locking himself inside.

Pulling out his cellphone, he dialed Zane and explained his situation, what had occurred, and where he was, and he pleaded with him to get someone over to protect Camilla and the children as soon as possible.

"Stay on that train no matter what. It's the only way we can help you," Zane said. "There has to be somebody on the inside that sold out your location. That's the only way your cover could have been blown."

"Must be a dirty cop," Will said. "Santiago has his fingers in the pot everywhere. I'm doomed. I may as well just go out and stand in the middle of the concourse and let them have me. I don't see any way out," he said sounding broken.

"Don't do anything stupid. Keep your phone close. I'll be back in touch," Zane said, hanging up.

Will quickly contacted Camilla to make sure she and the children were safe inside their condo. "I was just walking up to our building when I spotted two men just as they saw me. I knew they were out of place and my suspicions were correct. They gave chase and I ran all the way to the train station, which is where I'm hiding now. My train is about to leave."

"Will, where are you?" she asked.

"I just told you, I'm at the Amtrak station. The trains about to pull out."

"No, I mean what train are you on?" she asked with apparent concern.

"Listen, I don't have time to fill you in on the whole story, I have to go now. They were on my tail and are probably already on board this train now. I love you, Camilla. I'll be in touch. Keep the doors locked until you are sure it's the cops on the other side of the door. Make them prove it," he said, hanging up.

Just then, there was pounding on the bathroom door. "Hey, is anyone in there? I gotta go dude," a man complained. "You've been in there for ten minutes."

"I'm sick. Go away. Find another bathroom," Will said.

There was sudden kicking at the door, and Will knew who was on the other side. This time the messengers voice sounded much more menacing, "Come on out, Will. There is nowhere to hide. We know where your family is. Your beautiful wife, those three darling children...you wouldn't want to be responsible for their pain and suffering ...now would you? Quit playing games, my patience is wearing thin."

"How can I be sure you won't harm my family anyway?" Will asked.

"You're just going to have to trust me, aren't you? You have no choice. Don't be stupid," the voice said reasonably.

"How did you find us?" Will asked.

The man on the other side laughed. "Trust me you really don't want to know." Just then, the train whistle blew, and they pulled out of the station.

❧

"We tracked a call from Camilla's phone to Duvall's early this morning. We have reason to believe that Camilla is the one who gave up their cover." The officer explained to Zane and Darcy, "I'm sure there was a bargain involved, Will for her and her children's lives."

"That's cold," Darcy said.

"You got that right. Especially since they were not in any immediate danger," he replied.

"Why do you think she ratted them out?" Darcy wondered.

"Who knows, divided loyalty, protecting her babies, fear. Fear and paranoia will make you do strange things you wouldn't normally even consider," the officer said. "I've seen it all."

"Poor Will," Darcy said.

"When I just spoke with him, his only concern was for his family. He was ready to sacrifice himself and turn himself in to Santiago. I tried to reason with him. I'm not sure I convinced him though," Zane said. "I hope I was successful. He doesn't deserve this. His children deserve to grow up with their father," he said

⁓

Will decided that his only option was to walk out the door and turn himself in. He couldn't bear to think of his family suffering at the hands of these monsters. If it was the last thing he ever did, so be it. As he exited the bathroom, he was roughly grabbed, and a gun was jabbed into his ribcage, causing him to wince. "Now, remember, I will have a gun pointed at you the entire ride. I guess we're going to discover Toledo together," the man chuckled darkly.

"Where is your better half?" Will asked, showing a little gumption and sarcasm.

"We decided I could handle this on my own," he said. "No need to waste time and money on an extra ticket since you were basically trapped on board. Let's go take a seat. You have about four hours to think about your life and to pray for forgiveness for all of your sins," he laughed, nudging Will forward.

With resignation, Will moved forward like a dead man walking. He was still pondering what the man had said about him not wanting to know who had given up their location. He was in denial, and he managed to tamp down the slight niggling at the tip of his consciousness. Taking a window seat, the man slid in next to him, effectively blocking Will's exit.

~

Camilla let the tall gangly police officer in after demanding to see his I.D. through the peephole. He entered and sat down on the couch, and her children, who had never met a stranger, proceeded to entertain their new friend.

"Have you ever played 'I see something in the room'?" Daniel asked the officer. Isabella stared at him with her large brown eyes, nodding at everything her big brother said.

"Yes, I have, that is a great game," the officer said.

"The other tall man and pretty lady taught us how to

play when we were at the motel before." Daniel smiled. "I won."

"I too win," Isabella said, with dimples showing.

"Well, that's pretty special. I need to talk with your mom about some grown-up stuff right now. Can you watch your little sister while we go in the other room for a few minutes?" he asked Daniel.

"Sure, I can, because I'm a big boy," Daniel said proudly.

"Yes, you are. We will be right back, big guy."

The officer asked Camilla to sit at the dining room table, and he pulled up a chair close to her. "Tell me how it happened?" he asked.

"Will called and told me that when he approached our apartment building there were two men waiting for him. He fled to the train station and was boarded on a train getting ready to depart," she said.

"No, Camilla, tell me how they found your hideout?" he asked gently.

Wringing her hands, Camilla asked, "What do you mean?"

"I think you know what I mean," the officer answered.

She started crying silently, her shoulders shaking, and her head lowered. "They called me on my cellphone a week ago and told me that my brother wanted to give me a message. If I would tell him our location, my children and I would never be bothered again, and, in fact, Santiago would guarantee our protection for the rest of our lives. He told Christian to tell me that, if I didn't turn Will over to them, he could no longer protect me or my babies. We would be on our own," she said.

"I agonized for my husband. I love Will, I didn't know what to do," she said with a sob. "Christian said to make it easy on everyone. My choices were either to turn Will over to them or to know that my babies wouldn't live to see their next birthday. They threatened me that if I told Will or anyone else that when they discovered our safe house, and it was only a matter of time before they would, we would all suffer." She finally broke down completely, wailing with grief, guilt, and remorse.

The children, hearing their mother crying, came into the room with frightened eyes. Isabella ran to her mother and hugged her legs saying, "Mama cry. Why Mama cry?"

"Mama, are you sad?" Daniel asked, beginning to cry himself. Big tears welled in Isabella's eyes as she watched her brother becoming upset.

Camilla opened her arms and gathered her children against her chest, burying her nose in their hair. Kissing them both on the tops of their heads, she said with desperation in her voice, "Mama loves her babies so much. You both know that, don't you?"

"Mama, Mama, peese don't kwy. We wuv you." Isabella tried her best to communicate her worry, her chubby little arms squeezing her mother's legs.

"Mama, where is Daddy?" Daniel asked, with tears running down his cheeks. "I'm scared, Mama."

"It's going to be alright, kids," the police officer said kindly. "Your mommy was just a little scared, but she is strong and brave, just like you are, and it's going to be alright. You have to help each other. Deal?" he asked gently. "I'm going to make sure that you are all safe and ready for Santa. Have you written a letter to Santa yet?"

"Santa" was the magic word. Their expressions immediately lit up, and they began to tell him what they had asked for in their letters to the big man in the red suit. They looked up at their mother for reassurance, and Camilla had managed to gather herself for the sake of the kids and she smiled shakily at them.

"Yes, we've been waiting for Santa, haven't we? My babies have been so good. Santa definitely has them on his 'nice' list," Camilla said.

"We have an officer stationed at the entrance on the ground floor and one outside your door. Don't let anyone in unless they show you their identification card through the peephole, just like you did for me," the man cautioned.

"When will we know about Will?" Camilla asked, starting to collapse in emotion again.

"I'll contact you the minute he arrives in Toledo and we have him in our protective custody. As difficult as it will be, please try not to dwell on it, for your sake as well as your children's. Right now, all we can do is wait," he counseled. "My name is Officer Murphy, Rory Murphy. Here's my card. I'll be checking in on you ma'am. I'm so sorry this is happening to you and your family." He held out his freckled hand and she put her cold trembling hand in his and he squeezed.

"Thank you for not judging me," she answered quietly.

"But for the grace of God go I," Murphy responded. "It helps me to be able to sleep at night if I remember that." Turning to go, he said, "Take care, Ms. Havers."

CHAPTER 29

*T*hey were the longest four hours of Will's life. His captor, whom he had learned was named Jon, was a live wire ready to spark. He fidgeted and jumped in and out of his seat throughout the train ride to Toledo. Will thought he might be able to use this to his advantage if he could muster up the ability to give a damn. Jon looked practically green, and Will sensed there was something physical going on with him.

Will had almost given up when, suddenly, a picture of his children and Camilla entered his mind. He visualized them opening their presents Christmas morning. In that instant, he made the decision to give it one last shot if the opportunity presented itself.

"I've got to piss," Jon said crudely. "There's no place to hide, Will. If you're not sitting in that exact same spot when I return, you're a dead man." He hissed as he nervously looked around.

With resignation, Will replied, "I know that. I'll be

here."

"Your bro won't let you get away, you know. You may as well just face the music like a man and save your family. Although your wife doesn't have the same sense of loyalty to you that you seem to have for her." Jon grinned, enjoying witnessing Will's devastation as the last of his denial was stripped away. "She ratted you out. How do you think we found you?" he said, laughing as he rose unsteadily to go to the restroom. "You might want to think about that before you go risking your life to live happily ever after." Laughing at his own wit, he left Will alone.

Will felt like he was frozen to his seat. A sick realization formed as the pieces clicked together in his mind. He was shattered. Questioning what he had to live for, he once again pictured the faces of his three little ones, which compelled him to take another shot at survival. Despite Jon's warning, he knew there were plenty of places to hide on this train, especially if he could get to the lower level undetected. The sleeper cabins and the luggage storage areas were potential places to hide. And, by his estimation, they were only about fifteen minutes from Toledo. If he could remain undetected until they arrived, he had a shot.

Jumping from his seat, he hit the aisle at a run. He dashed through the door at the end of the car. The train jostled and holding on for balance, he stepped into the next car. He made his way to the sleeper section on the upper level. He looked into each cabin as he rushed by to see whether there were any empty ones to slip into. He decided to go forward to the next car before descending to the bottom level.

When he entered the next car, he practically dove down the first staircase he happened upon, the steep, narrow stairs leading to the bottom level of the train. Frantically searching for a perfect hiding spot, he ducked into a vacant sleeper compartment, slid the doors shut, and yanked the curtains closed. Pulling down the upper bunk, he crawled in, banging his head on the low ceiling as he tried to bury himself under the covers. He knew he had bought time because Jon would have to search each car and cabin to find him.

Upon returning a few short minutes later, Jon discovered the empty seat and was filled with fear and rage. Santiago would have his head if he screwed this up. His skin was crawling for another hit. He was beginning to feel the effects of withdrawal and cursed himself for his weakness. Things had happened so quickly at the train station, he never dreamed he would be boarding a train without the needed fix.

It was coming up on eight hours since his last hit of smack. He had been chasing the dragon for three years now, and Santiago had taken good care of him, making sure he never went without in exchange for his loyalty and labor. His skin was clammy, and his shakiness and restlessness were increasing by the minute. His trip to the bathroom had been more to ease his gastrointestinal discomfort he was having than to attend to his bladder. He had been fighting nausea for the last hour.

Wild-eyed, Jon erratically staggered down the aisle of the rocking car, waving his gun at the passengers as he went, demanding to know if they had seen a man with Will's description. Most shook their heads with expressions of terror, some screamed, some rose from their seats and ran the opposite direction. Chaos ensued.

As Jon was stepping through the door leading to the next car, a large, male passenger in full military uniform came from behind and tackled him to the ground, fighting for control of the gun. Jon was no match in his agitated state, and the hero easily contained Jon and gained possession of the firearm. "Call a conductor, and someone phone the Toledo police. Tell them we have a gun-wielding man contained and under control. Does anyone have a cord or something we can use to restrain him?" the uniformed passenger asked.

Jon was practically slobbering as he cursed and threatened the man sitting on top of him. "You'll be sorry you took it upon yourself to play the hero. I hope you have made peace with your maker. You're a dead man," he blathered.

"Shut the hell up before I knock you out," the soldier responded.

"You have no idea what you have unleashed upon yourself," Jon continued.

"Yeah, well, as you can see, I'm shaking in my boots. I faced a lot worse in Afghanistan than a strung-out junkie like you," he said.

A train employee arrived and informed everyone that the police had been notified and that they were on standby and waiting at the station. He thanked the passengers for remaining calm and thanked the soldier for his actions. "You are truly a hero," he commended. "The police will want your statement. We are just pulling into the station now. Please hang back while the other passengers disembark. We really appreciate what you did here," the attendant said effusively. The train car erupted in applause from his fellow passengers.

"He won't be such a hero when he is taking his last breath," Jon muttered.

~

*W*ill could tell the train had slowed down and was preparing to stop. He weighed his options. Stay hidden and wait until everyone had exited or make a run for it immediately. He knew that there would be cops crawling all over the station, so he thought it best to take his chances and exit immediately, then turn himself in for protection.

When the train came to a stop, Will waited for several minutes then crawled out from beneath the covers, banging his head again while trying to maneuver himself into position to get down from the upper bunk. Landing on his feet, he cautiously stuck his head out of the cabin and looked both ways, then made a run for it.

As he exited the train, he ran to the first police officer he saw. "Help me," he said desperately. "I'm Will Havers, and I'm in danger. I was held captive on the train from Chicago. I'm in witness protection and I was discovered, my cover blown. Help me please."

Will was quickly hustled out of the station and put in a waiting police cruiser. As he passed another police car, he saw Jon sitting in the back seat. Looking deranged and maniacal at seeing Will, he spat at the window, the glob of spittle making a slimy trail as it slid down the glass.

CHAPTER 30

Christian Silva had received the news that Will was alive and was pacing like a mad dog in his cell. *How could things have gotten so fucked up,* He had finally gotten through to his sister, only to have Will escape not once but two times. Jon was a dead man, he thought with little satisfaction. Christian knew that Santiago would be just as furious with him as he was with Jon. There was a slim chance that Santiago would cut him slack, he hoped that his loyalty and the fact that his hands were tied by his incarceration would be considered. He had gained his sister's location. He had no control over how it had played out. He hoped that it was enough for his boss.

It was time for the kitchen staff to begin dinner preparation, so he was led out by the guard to the mess hall. They all had their specific jobs on the line, so he immediately began to work at his tasks. Two hours later, the buffet was ready, and the prisoners filed in. He stood in front of the vegetable trays and scooped out portions on each plate thrust toward him.

A fight broke out at the far end of the cafeteria and pandemonium ensued. Fists were flying, bodies tumbling, food trays sailing across the room and being used as weapons. Suddenly, Christian was grabbed from behind and a deep voice whispered into his ear, "Santiago has a message for you. He said to tell you it's nothing personal." He felt something cold and sharp against his neck and then slumped to the floor, his throat cut from ear to ear, as a pool of his own blood grew around him. He lay there, gurgling, eyes open as the life drained from him. His last image was of his mama, smiling at him, holding her arms wide open for him to be enfolded in her embrace.

⁓

Zane and Will, safe and once again in protective custody, waited for Camilla and the children to disembark the plane. Will's family were flying back from Chicago this afternoon. It had been several days since her brother had been murdered in cold blood while a brawl distracted inmates and wardens alike. When Zane had told Will that his brother-in-law was dead, he had been shocked, but his relief had also been evident. There would be no trial to testify at except his own. On that front, Zane was optimistic that all charges would be dropped because, now that Christian was dead, Will's friend and employee had recanted yet again, switching back to his original testimony helping to clear the way for a dismissal. There just wasn't enough evidence for them to proceed with prosecution.

~

*C*amilla was so afraid. Would she be able to make Will understand why she behaved the way she had? Isabella and the baby were asleep, and Daniel was looking at a Christmas storybook with bright beautiful drawings of reindeer and elves and, of course, Santa himself.

"When will we see Daddy? Daniel asked.

"Very soon, my darling," Camilla said, sounding much calmer than she felt.

"I miss Daddy," he said.

"So do I." She put her arm around his slim shoulders and pulled him against her, kissing his head. "So do I," she repeated. Her emotions were going in a million different directions. Grief for her brother and his sad life and death, fear of losing her family and marriage, guilt and remorse for her cowardice, and a tiny sliver of hope that they could somehow overcome all of this to live a happy life together again, without fear for their lives.

They exited the plane with the help of a flight attendant, escorted by none other than Officer Rory Murphy, who carried Isabella and the carry-on bag so that Camilla could hold Daniel's hand while carrying the baby. They walked through the jetway leading to the terminal, where an employee waited with a double stroller for the babies.

She thanked the flight attendant and pushed the

stroller forward, with Daniel walking alongside her. Another officer waited to lead them out to the baggage claim area and transport them to the police station. Camilla was emotionally and physically running on empty. She was exhausted, with dark circles under her eyes, and was gray beneath her brown skin. She looked utterly defeated.

"Daddy!" Daniel took off running toward his father as he spied him at the end of the long airport atrium. Will stooped down on his haunches, waiting for his son with open arms.

"Daniel!" he shouted out, as he scooped the boy up into his arms, crying openly.

"Daddy, I missed you."

"Buddy, I've missed you, too."

Just then, Camilla reached Will, hesitant about what to do next. Will put Daniel back down and turned to her, searching deeply into her eyes. Satisfied with what he saw there, he pulled her into his arms and whispered, "I forgive you. You are the mother of my children and the love of my life." Camilla began to sob as she clung to Will, desperately holding on tight.

"Oh, Will, I'm so terribly sorry for betraying you," she said, hiccupping, with tears running down her ravaged face. "How can you ever forgive me or trust me again?" she wondered aloud.

"It's already done. I love you," he said simply. "Let's step into the rest of our lives together. We will heal from this, Camilla. You have to believe in love." He held her tight, and Daniel, too, who was crying as he gazed up at his father adoringly. Will's heart was full.

"Will Santa be able to find us here?" Daniel asked innocently.

Officer Murphy, standing close by said, "You bet he will, Daniel. Santa has superpowers." Rory Murphy, who had witnessed the exchange between Camilla, Will, and their son Daniel, had suspiciously over-bright eyes himself as he said, "Let's get back to the precinct so we can get you all settled for the night. I'm sure the kids are hungry."

Camilla smiled through her tears and thanked him. They made their way to the police van and headed back to the station to tie up any loose ends. Afterward, they would move into a condo, where they would stay temporarily until their own home could be professionally cleaned and made livable again. Zane knew that they would be happier having Christmas, which was only days away, in their own home so he paid extra to put a rush on the job.

Since Christian Silva was dead and Zane had just received word that the charges against Will had been officially dropped, there was reason to celebrate. With the danger to Will and his family resolved, there was no reason for Will to testify against Santiago, so they could safely return home as soon as it was ready.

Zane had enlisted Casey and Charlie to help him put up and decorate a tree, as well as to buy some toys for under the tree since they had to leave their Christmas presents behind in Chicago.

The best news for Zane was that Allie was flying back tomorrow. Allie had cried when he had given her the good news. She'd be getting home just in time for the office Christmas party.

CHAPTER 31

*A*llie sat on the toilet with her face in both hands in utter disbelief. She had peed directly on the stick and used all three tests that were in the kit she purchased several days ago. The results didn't change. The test read positive. She was pregnant. About four-and-a-half weeks pregnant. That was the first time she and Zane made love. The day after Thanksgiving. Now it was almost Christmas.

Before returning home from Florida, Allie had continued to battle with nausea. At first, she had refused to even consider she might be pregnant because she had gone on birth control pills right after they had made love the very first time. Denial was her friend. Until it wasn't.

That must have been all it took. One morning of lovemaking. When she was three weeks late with her period and nauseous, it began to sink in that maybe she needed to investigate further. She had assumed she was late from the emotional trauma of the attempted rape. Now, here she was all alone, sitting on the toilet, wondering what the hell she was going to do.

How would Zane react? She wasn't even sure how she felt. She had to admit there was fear, but even more present was an excitement. She could already feel a love for this miracle growing inside of her. She never thought it would happen again, but at thirty-eight she was more prepared than she had been in her early twenties. She knew she would keep the baby. Her hand trembled as she picked up the test with the pink positive sign. *What the hell, she was going to be a mom!*

~

That evening, Allie stood facing the bathroom mirror struggling to get a pair of dangly diamond earrings into her ears. Zane had surprised her with them and the diamond necklace she was already wearing. Coming up behind her, Zane said, "Here, let me." Taking the earrings, she moved so he could reach more easily, and he slipped the wires in. She turned back and met Zane's eyes in the mirror. He slipped his arms around her from behind and pulled her against his torso. She could feel he was becoming aroused, and it satisfied her at a deep level that she had such an effect on him.

She wore a silky black backless jumpsuit with wide pant legs and a low V neckline in the front. The jumpsuit had a silver chained belt that rested around her waist. The long necklace of white gold encrusted with diamonds rested below her breast-line. Her thick blonde hair shimmered and fell loosely around her shoulders and down her back. She had applied a smoky brown eyeshadow, which accented her large brown irises. She had decided to wear a dramatic rich red lipstick, which was stunning on her.

Zane wore an expensive, hand-tailored black suit with an Italian white point collared dress shirt with a French-placket button front. His tie for the evening was red-and-black striped, his nod to the Christmas festivities. His normally unruly black hair had been tamed down with a gel product, causing Allie to want to run her fingers through it and ruffle it up.

The Christmas party was being held at the country club. Since this would be their first official appearance as a couple, Allie was beyond nervous. Zane tried to reassure her that people wouldn't be surprised, and everyone would be happy for them. "They might feel sorry for you, Allie, and they will certainly be whispering about my dumb luck," he said, kissing her and nibbling on her ear before they made their entrance.

"I just hate being the center of gossip. You know we will be picked apart by some," she said.

"So what? It only comes from their insecurities. The people who matter, those who really know us, will be supportive and they're the ones that count."

"I know you're right," Allie said.

"Ready?"

"Ready as I'll ever be."

Zane opened the doors and they stepped into the ballroom. Heads turned as the stunning couple entered. They could have been walking the red carpet in Hollywood. Spying Allie, Annika came running up to her, throwing her arms around her friend and giving her a big hug. A server appeared with a drink tray, when Allie declined Zane raised his eyebrows in surprise, then selected a glass of white wine for himself.

"I have missed you so much." Eyes darting toward Zane, Annika said, "This one," nodding her head toward Zane, "was almost impossible to work with while you were gone." Since her friend Allie was there to have her back, she said bravely, "Thank God you're back."

Zane had the decency to look sheepish as he quickly apologized. "I can't say it's a lie. I'm working on my impatience and short-temperedness, but I have a long way to go. I'm sorry I've been so difficult lately."

"No problem, Zane," Annika said. "I've been with the firm a long time, and I know you're a good man. Otherwise I wouldn't let my friend here date you." She smiled, her beautiful white teeth sparkling against her rich deep skin. She wore a long, off-white sleeveless dress that flattered her flawless complexion. Her hair was done in dozens of small braids that must have taken hours to accomplish. The end result was a work of art.

Stella walked up, linking her arm through Annika's. "Hi, Mr. Dunn. Allie, you are breathtakingly beautiful. You are as well, Annika. You are both much more suited to Hollywood than a law office in Michigan," she said effusively.

"Hello, Stella. You look lovely yourself," Zane said, causing Stella to blush.

"Merry Christmas, Stella," Allie chimed in, giving her a quick hug.

"Are your son and his family coming home for the holidays?" Allie asked.

"Yes. They arrive the day before Christmas and will stay for a whole week. I'm so excited," Stella said.

Just then, one of the partners raised a glass and tapped it loudly with a spoon to gain everyone's attention. "Can I have your attention for a moment? I just want to welcome everyone and thank you all for making our firm one of the most successful and respected law firms out there. We couldn't do it without you all. Zane, do you have anything you would like to add?"

"I'm very grateful for each and every one of you. We're so much more than an office. We are family. I know the sacrifices you make when needed, the overtime and long hours you put in. I just want you to know, it doesn't go unnoticed. I'd like to make a toast to all of you. Here's to a prosperous coming year and health to you and all your loved ones. Merry Christmas everyone."

CHAPTER 32

*T*hey woke up early Christmas morning to a fresh cover of snow. Zane kissed Allie awake, then said, "I'll call you when breakfast is ready. Then I'd like to go out for a winter walk. What do you think?"

She stretched out sensuously, "Sounds lovely."

A half hour later Allie sat at the kitchen island ready to dig into a pile of fresh berries, served over French toast, dusted with powdered sugar and topped with local maple syrup.

"You know you're setting a dangerous precedent, don't you? I'm developing pretty high expectations."

Grinning Zane said, "Good thing I like to cook."

They were both unusually quiet as they finished breakfast. "I'll clean up. Why don't you go put on some winter clothes?"

"Winning!" Allie joked, as she jumped up to change

clothes. She was anxious to get outside and hoped the cold air would clear her head and calm her nerves.

The whole world seemed hushed and magical as they walked around the property. Zane held Allie's mittened hand and pointed out various critter tracks in the snow as they hiked along. Several woodpeckers clung to the suet cages hanging from his trees and birds hungrily vied for the seed at the feeder.

"It's so peaceful here. It feels like we're a million miles from anywhere," Allie said.

"Yes."

"You're awfully quiet this morning," Allie said.

"I was thinking the same about you. What's on your mind?"

"This and that. Just thinking about you and me," Allie said.

He stopped walking and turned to face her, "You aren't having doubts already are you?"

"No, nothing like that. Just wondering how you see us...you know..."

"How do *you* see us?"

Allie searched his eye's, squinting against the sun. "No fair answering a question with a question. I guess I was wondering, since we've never talked about it...do you see yourself with children?"

"I'm definitely not attached to the idea. Is that what you're worried about? It would be a major life disruption and I think things are pretty good the way they are." He brushed his gloved thumb across her rosy cheek, then leaned down and lightly pressed his lips to hers. He lifted his head and saw tears shimmering in her eyes. "Did I say something wrong?"

Allie's heart felt heavy. *Disruption.* Not the words she'd been hoping to hear. "No, I'm just feeling sentimental."

"Babe, I know how hard it was for you to lose your baby. I would never ask you to go through that again for me. I'm happy with the way things are. We've got each other and Kit Kat. Okay? No need to cry."

Suddenly surprise and relief transformed Allie's face. She held up her mittened hand, "Wait, so does this mean you wouldn't necessarily be opposed to the idea?"

Recognition suddenly dawned on his face as a few clues clicked together in his head. "Allie, do you have something you'd like to share with me?"

She looked down at her feet, took a deep breath, then said in a rush, "Zane I'm pregnant."

His eye's widened then a smile broke across his face. "*We're* pregnant?" She nodded her head yes. "How long have you known?"

"I just took the test the other day. I've been waiting for the right time to tell you. I wasn't sure how you'd feel about it. I'm not going to lie to you, when I just heard you say 'we' I finally took a breath."

"Oh my God! I'm going to be a dad!" He picked Allie up and swung her around. "We have so much to plan... so much to think about. What if it's a girl? What if it's a boy?"

Allie laughed. "Well it's bound to be one or the other."

His eye's burned with passion as he looked at her, "If it's a girl she won't be driving until she's twenty-one or dating until she's thirty."

"You're going to be a great dad and if it's a girl she'll have you wrapped around her little finger."

"Just like someone else I know," he said. "Let's go inside, I don't want you to catch a chill in your condition."

"I'll be fine. The fresh air is good for us."

He suddenly looked serious as he gripped her arms, "Babe, I won't let you or our baby down. I promise I've got you both."

Her eye's sparkled, "There is no doubt in my mind. I've seen you in action. Now about that nap..."

CHAPTER 33

*L*ater as they lay watching an old classic movie, Allie yawned loudly and said, "I feel so lazy."

"Today, I'm completely at your command, you don't even have to get off this couch," he said.

"You'd better be careful about what you say, I can be quite demanding."

"Don't I know it." He comically raised his eyebrows up and down, twisting an imaginary handlebar mustache.

Allie giggled. "Let's just lay around together all day and watch movies."

"Deal," he said.

Zane rolled on top of Allie and began pressing his hardness against her pelvis. Leaning down to kiss her soft lips, he gently encouraged them open as their arousal deepened. He began to press harder and rubbed his erection against her, the friction making her wet with desire. He pulled her T-shirt up and bent down to take her nipple into his mouth. Sucking gently at first, as she bucked underneath him, he began to suckle her breast in earnest as if he were drinking of her nectar. As he pulled and tugged with his lips and tongue, he fondled her other breast, Allie was almost delirious with passion.

He pushed himself up and pulled her top over her head and threw it aside. He then began to pull her sweatpants down over her hips and thighs. Reaching her ankles, he tugged them the rest of the way and tossed them to the ground. He paused to gaze at the perfection that was Allie. Her belly still flat but soon to be swelling with their growing baby, her beautiful full breasts, ripe and slightly swollen from the pregnancy, her flushed face, her plump moist lips, eyes soft and slightly glazed with wanting. He tugged at her lacey panties, pulling them down the length of her long legs until they landed on the growing heap of clothing. He slid back up to kiss her again.

"Allie, you don't know what you do to me. I can't ever seem to get enough of you," He murmured while snuggling up beside her, so he could pleasure her further. Reaching between her legs, he found her wet center and plunged his finger into her deeply as his thumb rubbed against her sweet spot. He bent down to take her areola into his mouth while quickening the rhythm of his finger, thrusting in and out of her vagina. He removed his fingers—causing Allie to moan, "Don't stop!"—only so he could pull his boxer shorts off. He kissed her as she spread her legs wider, welcoming him. Gently, he began to move inside her as he hungrily kissed her. Increasing his tempo, he pumped wildly, thrusting in and out of her wet entry as Allie panted with need. She exploded in an orgasm that went on and on for several minutes of ecstasy. He was close behind her, moaning her name aloud as he felt wave after wave while ejaculating inside her pulsating vagina.

After the waves had subsided, she held his penis in her hand, gently cupping him. They both fell into a light sleep. Allie woke up first, aroused by his sexy body lying next to her. She straddled him, waking him up by planting kisses all over his face. Her belly flip flopped as she looked at his muscular chest and sculpted abdomen. Waking, he gasped with pleasure as she ran her fingers over his chest, exploring the contrast between steely muscles and soft hair. She then moved further down to feel the wiry hair above his penis, massaging his pubic bone. Smiling at his quick response, she began to pull his shaft like she was milking it.

He groaned as if in pain, "Allie, are you trying to kill me?" She kissed her way down as he opened his muscular thighs wider, the soft hair on his legs a pleasing sensation against her cheeks, as she cupped his testicles, fondling them gently while continuing to nuzzle him between his legs. She loved the musky manly smell of him.

When she was sure he was at his peak, she positioned herself over him, straddled and inserted his manhood into her warm wet center, and began to ride him hard. His large penis filled her completely. She rubbed against him, wiggling as he pulsated inside her. His breath quickened as heat built within. She fingered his nipples, nestled in the dark hair of his chest.

He was mesmerized by her breasts, swaying and

bouncing as she rode harder and harder. He reached up to fondle her ample bosom, causing Allie to throw her head back in unrestrained abandon. As she arched, her long blond hair cascaded down her back and around her shoulders. She increased her rhythm and he bucked underneath her as they both climaxed together.

Afterward, as he lay with his head on her belly, lips against her skin, he said softly, "Hey, Little One, how was the ride?"

"Zane, you are terrible," Allie said, giggling as she swatted at his head.

He grinned mischievously, eyes sparkling with merriment. "Well weren't you wondering the same thing?" he asked.

"Absolutely not," she said primly.

"Yeah, sure you weren't." He began to tickle Allie, causing her to laugh out loud and try to squirm out from under him. "Tell the truth."

"OK, I actually did think of it... after, you know...." She dissolved into laughter. "Is this what it is going to be like for the next seven months?"

"We'll get used to it, I'm sure," he said. Kissing her belly, he said with his lips against her bare skin, "Merry Christmas, baby. We can't wait to meet you. You are going to have the best mommy ever. We love you so much." Allie smiled down at Zane, stroking his hair back from his brow.

"I've got a surprise for your mama," he whispered conspiratorially.

He pushed himself up and went over to the credenza, opening a drawer while Allie admired his bare backside. Her gaze wandered over his strong muscular shoulders and back, leading to a narrow waist and toned buttocks and thighs. What a view.

Reaching in, he pulled out a small box. He returned and kneeled on the floor next to Allie. Opening the jeweler's box, he removed a two-carat diamond engagement ring. He stared intently into Allie's wide eyes. "Allie, I love you with every fiber of my being. Will you marry me?"

Her eyes welled up, "Oh my God! It's beautiful, Zane," she murmured, marveling at the large sparkling diamond nestled in delicate white gold filigree. She held out her hand and he slipped the ring onto her finger. Wrapping her arms around his neck, she pulled him against her naked breasts. "Yes! I love you, too, Mr. Dunn, and I want to spend the rest of our days discovering just how deep we can go."

He wiped the tears with his thumb and kissed her where her tears had been. "It's you and me, Babe. For the long haul. You will never get rid of me. We're going to be one heck of a team. Next year at this time, we'll have a bundle we can hold. Can you believe it?" he asked in wonderment.

Just at that moment, as if not wanting to be left out of the love fest, Kit Kat made an entrance grumbling to herself, reminding them that they already had a bundle to hold.

"Kit get over here," Zane said, encouraging her to join them by patting the couch cushion. She jumped up immediately and began to purr as Zane and Allie showered her with affection.

"We didn't mean to leave you out, girl. You're going to love this new bundle as well," Zane said. Kit Kat rubbed her whiskers against his hand, rolled onto her back, and stretched out full length, the ultimate sign of trust.

"You certainly have her under your spell," Allie commented.

"I love being adored," he said grinning.

"Well, you don't have to travel far to find your own set of groupies. We reside right under your roof." She laughed as Kit stared adoringly up at Zane, proving her point.

"Zane, I just want you to know that I can hardly wrap my head around all that has happened. Throughout this whole terrifying ordeal, you have shown bravery, strength, and compassion. You're so much more than I could ever have hoped to find in a mate. You're not only my mate, but my friend, my confidante, my lover, my muse. I can't wait to see you as a father, and there is no one besides you I would rather go on that journey with."

"Allie, I'm no hero. It was completely selfish on my part, because I simply couldn't have gone on if I had lost you. I honestly didn't believe that a love like ours could exist. All the poetry and love songs and stories seemed like works of fiction and overactive imaginations, but now I know the truth about love. It's real and the most precious gift of all," he said humbly.

Allie gazed at her fiancé, feeling almost overwhelmed by his openness, decency, and depth. "I have to keep pinching myself, I'm so happy right now," she said, as the three of them, plus baby, covered themselves up in a crocheted afghan.

"Merry Christmas," Allie sighed with contentment, eyes already getting heavy.

"Merry Christmas."

The End...for now

I hope you enjoyed reading More Than A Boss as much as I enjoyed writing it.

Please click on the following link to read More Than A Memory, book two of The Heartland series. There is also a link to my readers group. Thanks for reading!

Universal Link: mybook.to/MoreThanAMemory

https://www.facebook.com/groups/179183050062278/

ACKNOWLEDGMENTS

I would like to thank Merek Ramirez for connecting me to Holly Hudson, who then connected me with April Wilson, who is one of the most generous people I have come across. I also want to thank my editor Laura Carlson whose gentleness and skill were invaluable. A huge shout out to Julie Hopkins of Indie Book Cover Design for her artistry and kindness.

Printed in Great Britain
by Amazon